OH WI...

First published ... title *Cruelle Zé...* ... ...ous erotic novel crea... ...ite a controversy and gained a fair measure of critical attention. It is here presented in its first English language edition in a translation by Celeste Piano who is noted for her work on several novels by Emmanuelle Arsan.

OH WICKED COUNTRY!

Anonymous

Translated by Celeste Piano

Star

A STAR BOOK

published by
the Paperback Division of
W. H. ALLEN & Co. Ltd

A Star Book
Published in 1982
by the Paperback Division of
W. H. Allen & Co. Ltd
A Howard and Wyndham Company
44 Hill Street, London W1X 8LB

Copyright © Société Nouvelle des Éditions
Jean-Jacques Pauvert 1978
Translation copyright © Star Books 1982

Typeset by V & M Graphics Ltd, Aylesbury, Bucks
Printed in Great Britain by
Hunt Barnard Printing Ltd., Aylesbury, Bucks.

ISBN 0 352 31035 9

OH WICKED COUNTRY!

The most general form of happiness consists of not knowing that one is unhappy.

Frank and I were married in 1837, Coronation Year. Over the next few years we remained in England, either in London, Bath or at the modest Scottish estate of Frank's parents, the McLeods, and during this time it never occurred to me that I was particularly unhappy nor, for that matter, the converse. Yet one always believes the same applies to everybody else, to people one knows and even more so to those one does not.

Only once did Frank greatly displease me. I refer of course to what happened on our wedding night. It so happened that against all the odds I had been quite well-informed as to what men did to women. Some of my friends at boarding school used to discuss such matters, in more or less veiled but occasionally forthright terms. My mother herself had deemed it prudent to broach the subject shortly before that wretched night when I found myself alone with Frank. So I was not too disconcerted. But I still found it most disagreeable. However scrupulous the preparation, one really cannot imagine those movements, that sensation, or the sudden grunt a man makes.

1

Previously I had always found Frank delightful. I liked the fact that he was tall, and I liked his guards officer's uniform and his aroma of leather and cigars. I readily excused his absurdities because they amused me. He kissed me on the lips as soon as we were betrothed. And although this strangely disturbed me, as if my own father had caught sight of my nakedness, I nevertheless preferred him to kiss me upon the mouth. When he kissed my cheek, or ventured to kiss me as he sometimes did, above the tight collar of my dress where my neck was exposed, he would take the opportunity to brush his own cheek against my skin. His moustache, side-whiskers and luxuriant beard prickled far more than they tickled; I dreaded contact of this sort for I have very smooth sensitive skin and I always felt he would graze me, leaving marks and scars.

Then suddenly there was no longer anyone to chaperone me, no one to keep me from Frank nor to make him keep his distance.

Picture a great room in a manor house buffeted by the winds of Scotland. The jovial wedding guests had departed. Frank's and my parents had decided, as if it were some sort of game, to spend the night in the hunting lodge, a mile or two from the big house. I did not know where the servants slept and I was not even permitted to have a chambermaid attend me. I washed in an adjoining room, without examining myself (I have always done thus, not staring at myself overmuch for that usually embarrasses me). Following my mother's advice I washed as meticulously as I could. I did not fully understand the particular need for I am always extremely clean (it's a matter of upbringing) but I took her advice to heart. I went to bed and waited for a while and then Frank appeared. Or was it indeed he?

My eyes, accustomed to the darkness, made him out fairly clearly. But where were his gleaming boots, his spurs, his sabre? Dear God, men's bare calves and feet were frightful! And where was that manly, open expression at once ingenuous and mysterious? Why was he laughing nervously?

He approached the bed, placed one knee upon it, and waited as I too waited. But I could do nothing, say nothing. Finally he lifted a corner of the sheet and blankets and lay down as if alone. His weight so altered the disposition of the bed that I was forced towards him as if sliding down a river bank. With all my might I clung on, inert. If only he would speak. But he said nothing. Then he repeated my name foolishly: 'Stella! Stella! Stella!'

I was seized by the wild fancy that it was he who was crying out for help. Heavens, how I despised him! It seemed to me that I could sense - without even touching him - the frightening, hateful smell of his body. I thought I heard Frank, the man I called Frank, snigger once more. I realised what he was going to do yet at the same time I could scarcely imagine it - one would have thought I knew nothing at all! At that moment I realised the true meaning of loneliness.

Frank was breathing heavily. For fear of making as much noise as he, I held my own breath until I almost suffocated and asphyxia made my ears buzz and my temples throb. But all this fear and

Oh Wicked Country

these exteme emotions were quite useless since he, being the man, knew what he wanted and how he was going to get it. He thought only of his own animal lusts and had neither time to waste nor sensitivity to spare on a young girl shuddering in panic.

'Stella, Stella!' he cried.

Why did he repeat the name when he obviously didn't care who I was? He might just as well have said Mary or Grace, for I understood that I was not important to him. He called my name again and I did not reply. How could I trust someone who had me at his mercy and who scared me so? Then, still grinning and sniggering, he leaned over me and one of his hands, like a beastly claw, crushed my bosom, clutching hard at my breasts. Once my mother had remarked that I had very pretty breasts. Were they solely for the delectation of this male claw? With his other hand Frank pulled up my long nightgown. I so wished that I were not naked beneath it. Yet I was, and it appeared I was not to be allowed one single garment to protect myself. He pulled the nightgown up past my knees, past my thighs and then over my stomach. I so wanted to have no sex, to have none of that shocking fur, those lips, that intimate opening, that fissure. I wanted to be tight-shut, as clean as a child. But it was too late. Was Frank going to strip me completely?

No. He left the nightgown crumpled up above my stomach, for it was not I myself, nor even my body with its delicate smooth skin, which mattered to him. He was only interested in that wretched accident, that meeting-place of thighs and stomach,

4

which made me precisely what then I was not, a woman, a female - just like all the rest. I underwent such shame and disgust that I closed my legs as tightly as I could in order to hide myself, to forget the fact. But as for him, that and that alone was the very spot where he wished to despoil and enter, to uncover and undo me. He muttered and thrust his hand between my thighs until I was obliged to yield. I am even more sensitive in that place than upon my breasts, which nonetheless curiously harden sometimes and extend as if themselves hungry. However, it was my vulnerability itself, which was exciting this man I thought I loved. As soon as I had, despite myself, half-opened my thighs, his fingers curved and grasped me at that precise place, crushing me like a flower. There, he had discovered my most helpless, weakest spot, the very place where I was utterly open, and he worked away at it with a horrid contentment.

He now knew that beneath my clothes and for all my human dignity and maidenly modesty, there existed at one part of my otherwise irreproachable body this different variety of flesh, furled yet secretly yawning, fragile and, above all, damp. He deliberately plunged his finger straight into this intolerable humidity, this unbearable cavity, sinking it inside me as if penetrating and probing my very soul. I tried with all my strength to contract and resist, but my mind and will were detached from my body. On its shameful course the man's finger encountered I know not what obstacle or barricade, and it caused me dreadful pain, but I dared not scream, and he, by contrast, was still grunting with satisfaction. I thought he might yell out with pleasure. Despite myself I thrust down a hand so as to protect myself, to hide and prohibit that hole, that wound. The man removed his finger from the depths of my tender opening and took my hand. The wetness from within me was upon his finger and I wished I were dead.

Yet what did *he* want? Brutally he directed my own hand, forcing it against himself, against his nightshirt, then upon a clustered mass of hairs and suddenly on the strange object projecting from his body. It was raised up and round, burning hot and throbbing yet rigid. Now I knew what he, the man, also hid beneath his clothes and his smiling, gentlemanly manner. I felt nauseated: I was frightened, frozen. I wrenched my hand away to disengage myself, to avoid touching the revolting body of a man.

How ugly and vulgar it all was! As for him, however, he was laughing. In order to prevent my closing my thighs again he wedged his knee between them, then the length and full weight and force of the whole leg. He lay full-length over me and at the same time tried to support himself upon his forearms, arching his back as if intending to draw back. His right hand had let go my breast, and he rested his whole weight on his left elbow. Then the free hand again descended, hesitated one might almost say. It returned with the same feverish yet stubborn hesitation to my loins, slid inside me once more as if to ensure that I had not managed to contract myself again, emerged, seemed to busy itself – this time about the man's own stomach – and suddenly I understood that along with his hand and into this last intercrural conduit, between the lips of my sex, within its very interior, was another, longer, swollen cumbersome finger. I was well aware that this was his body's own individual sex. He would never manage to insert this, I would not permit him, neither of us could want this - and I struggled to block all entry. Then I tried to expel him and expel was the word, since it was too late to deny admission. The man had well and truly succeeded in introducing within me the head of this extra digit, this monstrous stave, and it was stretching me till I felt I would simultaneously both split and scream. A single obstacle halted it, the same one which had recently kept his actual finger at bay. I thought the man would give up, take this loathsome object out of me as he had his finger. But no, dear God! Quite the contrary - he persisted, pushing it violently inside me with all his strength!

He was going to tear me apart, I could feel it, I was sure of it, and I bit my lip viciously so as not to scream. Then with one thrust he did indeed tear me open: it was like a tiny inner explosion, a darting yet heavy pain. I experienced suffering not actually unbearable but so unjust, so undeserved that hatred made me gnash my teeth. As for him, that man, the monster - as if he had caused me no harm and all this were nothing and I did not even exist - he continued rubbing inside me, in my most private zone, ploughing his stubborn way blindly into my vitals. He must have been happy indeed, for he had won, had succeeded in forcing that gigantic and stupid male appendage of his completely inside me, inside my very core of being. This foreign body burned and filled and split me, it was rending me in twain and the two parts would never again mend.

He meanwhile appeared relieved and happy enough. He toyed with me, pretending to withdraw before plunging back again, then he feigned to dally only to speed furiously as though making up for his dawdling. He thrust home anew, sinking deeper and moving ever faster until at length he immersed himself a last time as deeply as he was able. Then, utterly swollen, he bucked at my loins and in an inexplicable frenzy burst out twitching and gasping and flooded me inside with blood and tears. *My* blood and *my* tears. The man grunted like an animal. It was the height of absurdity, for anyone might have thought that *his* soul was being snatched from him, that it was he who was wounded, he who wept! I was nothing more than a shred of flesh, a scrap of spirit - the living, suffering remnant of a human being. The extended, relaxed body of the man still lay heavily upon mine however, crushing me with its weight. I would have given anything in the world to have been able to lift him off me, to free myself and run to wash with rough flannel and hard brushes, scrubbing myself as if my salvation depended on it. But even that much I could not do. The man's inexorable weight bruised me. I realised that with his exploit accomplished and himself relieved of whatever had been burdening his own body, he had finally fallen asleep.

The next day Frank was once again well-dressed

and had the semblance of a civilised person, resembling in fact the man I had known hitherto and thought I loved. He nevertheless had the good sense never to mention that night. There was no doubt that he knew well enough that his behaviour had displeased me and that I would not forget it. But he affected to have forgotten it. I suppose it can be said that we all live upon such terms, more or less.

During the next few years, as I explained, we were happy enough or at any rate I never imagined we were not. I was fortunate in that I never had to bear Frank's child. I would not have relished this and perhaps indeed I might have found it intolerable. For truly that would have made Frank too much a part of me. That ridiculous engine of his was quite sufficient: for in fact Frank regularly persisted in coming to visit me when I was about to retire and in cramming it between my thighs. It hardly caused me any further pain, however, and scarcely vexed me. I accepted that most married men behaved thus, after all. Anyhow, Frank soon stopped. Perhaps he himself also attached little importance or interest to it and was only conforming to what was expected of a husband. As soon as he entered my room I would lie upon my back and would even go so far - out of a sort of pity for Frank - as myself to draw up my long shift past my stomach and to part my thighs.

He would habitually begin by handling or palpating me, always in identical places, his right hand on my left breast, his left hand betwixt my thighs. He would penetrate me with a finger, always in the same way it seemed, as if to

9

reconnoitre the terrain and assure himself that in the darkness my sex had not moved to the small of my back nor been displaced behind one of my ears. This tentative yet systematic examination horrified me, but it did not last long. The finger gave place to his blunt, witless lengthy appendage. I had seen the thing one night when the room was unusually light and Frank, erect like some lewd street-urchin was outlined clearly as he moved towards me. It reminded me of a swollen-wattled turkey stupidly inflating its comb. After introducing this inside me, Frank toiled on with embarrassed haste, groaning and flailing about for a short while, then he would pant, give vent to his usual little gasp, and withdraw, spent. Before he had left the room or even my bed I would run and wash furiously in the antechamber. I used to dream of a world where men, and people in general, would remain always fully-clad and be well-bred and polite. By the time I returned to bed Frank would be back in his own room. The following day we would never mention it. We could then begin to live like normal human beings once again.

I never discovered the precise reason for Frank's disgrace, nor why the regiment posted him to what amounted to exile among those Godforsaken islands. He drank, of course, but no more than other officers. Perhaps it had to do with gaming – he had lost too much money or on the contrary had won just a little too much! At any rate it was of no great importance to me, as soon as I learned officially that his honour would not be besmirched. His commanding officers' version of the reason for his posting abroad was that the natives in the South Seas were proving rebellious and this insurrection would have to be put down by force. It was also bruited about that the French had colonial designs upon the newer territories and the latter would have to be claimed post haste.

Various settlers, banded together in a sort of league calling itself the New Zealand Association, were engaged in putting pressure on the Government, and therefore on the Army also, to act upon the matter. It is common knowledge that shopkeepers rule nations. As far as I was concerned, I had a foreboding when Frank first mentioned to me those very gutters of the Empire, Australia in particular. To me it was nothing but a land of convicts. No proper society could exist out there, while a lady or even a gentleman would never be able to adapt to it. Frank explained to me that we were not exactly going to Australia itself, which is in any case a continent and not an island. It was a case of going further afield still, to remoter and more distant lands. New Zealand. And after all why not, since in a certain respect my life, our life together, was itself isolated, lost? Out there, so far from London, and from all things civilised, at least we would comprise an outpost of progress instead of being its very backwater.

11

Oh Wicked Country

There are no cities out there, only small settlements, rudimentary landing-stages, way-stations, trading posts, encampments. At the end of an interminable and insanitary voyage we landed at one such place in Australia. The handful of whites who stagnate there call it Sydney.

Then, after a second, shorter sea-voyage, we reached Wellington, New Zealand. Curiously, the truth about the reason for Frank's posting had preceded us even there: doubtless word had got out on the voyage, but the few true blue English folk stranded in those deserts christened with the names of towns all cold-shouldered us. So Frank, myself and a small cavalry escort left almost immediately, heading for the northern region of the island. Wellington itself stands on the northerly peninsula, but we were going still further north, beyond Napier, somewhere between what is called East Cape and the outposts of Hamilton and Auckland, into the Rotorua district. We knew that the settlers there were having grave clashes with the natives. But I never did know the exact destination of Frank and the few soldiers under his command.

In the hill country, in the midst of the bush that extends from the river Waikato as far as Lake Rotorua, we were attacked by a horde of Maoris, swarming as if by magic down from trees steaming with damp in the sun, who flung themselves recklessly upon our small band. I no longer recollect that battle very well. Half naked blacks, who at first yelled with wild defiance or anger, thereafter rushed silently about under the huge mist-veiled sun, whirling spears and war clubs. I

12

saw the purplish stain of a wound on a soldier's bright tunic. I also saw Frank fall from his horse. One of his heels caught in the stirrup and his steed dragged him for some way thus. But then I felt a blow just below the nape of my neck and I lost consciousness.

The golden light of the South Seas, filtered by the continual rain and taking on the green tinge of the foliage, illumined the outlines of a kind of hut (*whare*, I would learn, was the correct word) and finally reached me. These rays divided all of the hut into thick bars of shadow alternating with diffused radiance. I felt very hot, I was damp and extremely dirty, while a dull, somehow distant pain sounded like a gong inside my head.

Without quite knowing why, I dared not move. I was stretched out upon a bed, or rather, as I realised when touching it, a sort of very low palliasse consisting of four short stakes for its feet, a frame of branches or thin polished poles, and a network of lianas itself covered by a mattress of leaves. I immediately resisted the temptation to weep or utter any cry for help. At the same time it occurred to me that Frank and the soldiers must have been taken prisoner, like myself, or else were dead. Otherwise I should have heard their voices, or rifle shots or some sort of noise. It seems a trifle improper to confess that I felt a pressing call of nature. Yet I could summon no resolution to rise and satisfy it, any more than I had been able to cry out. In any case I should not have known where to go.

In addition to this I was terribly hungry, and the

throbbing sensation from the blow or bruise at the back
of my head was growing to fever-pitch. Under the
circumstances, my recollection of that time was of
nausea mingled with anxious apprehension. Whole
hours disappeared in brief moments, seemingly, or
were taken up by a single dizzying movement or
some minutiae of my attention or awareness. The
reverse also happened, whereby a minute or
perhaps a second were expanded infinitely, fluidly,
assuming an opaque identity like the quality of
fever itself or of nightmare. Nature's little needs, to
use my governess's childhood phrase, dragged me
out of this stuporous state and gradually restored
me to consciousness. I tried to control myself so
desperately that at times I felt a burning sensation at
the base of my womb, where Frank would always
sink his finger. Then just when I could no longer
hold back and was about to relieve myself, my
whole body stiffened and I forgot my stabbing need.
I distinguished a new noise, some chatter, some
footsteps.

'Frank?' I said. Where we in England would have
set the door there was a large screen of foliage. A
huge rectangle of light suddenly spilt into the hut
and in the centre of it several creatures – women,
judging by their breasts – were gesticulating. Five
or six of them had all entered together without the
slightest hesitation or embarrassment. The light
which I had at first found so dazzling now seemed
less bright, either because my fever-ridden eyes were
accustoming themselves to it or because the day was
waning and evening already drawing on. I caught
sight of the grey-blue sky and the green swaying

14

palms and all the abundant vegetation upon the hills behind the women. They, like the men who had attacked us, were almost naked. A short loincloth, or rather a strip of material – white for most of them, vividly coloured for a few – was tightly swathed around their private parts. The rest of their bodies, torsos, arms, thighs and legs were quite uncovered. They had long black hair, apparently clean and beautifully shiny (if, that is, one can find beauty in savages), and skin and flesh of a remarkable sheen no doubt due to their custom of going about naked. Their legs, however, were much scored by the undergrowth, up to the tops of their thighs. The kind of tightly wound cloth they wore began almost at the navel but in fact barely covered that. I do not know if the sounds issuing from their mouths could be construed as language, although it was not actually a disagreeable noise. There were many vowels and few consonants, something akin to the babbling of infants.

The women surrounded me, chattering and jabbering. Some of them without more ado sat upon what served as my bed, and all stared at me, scrutinising me with their huge black sparkling eyes that resembled olives. I was well aware that one must never show fear in such company. The bizarre creatures seemed to be asking questions of me in their *lingua franca*. I did not venture to understand them, nor did I have any intention, moreover, of trying to do so. The smiles of some of them, just like the cold, severe inquisitorial expressions of others among them, left me equally unmoved. Or rather, equally defiant.

'Where is Frank? Where is Captain McLeod?' I enquired of them. 'I should also be obliged if you brought me something to drink as soon as possible!'

They fell to chattering again, but it seemed to me that they were no longer addressing me but simply conferring amongst themselves. And the moment I believed they were going to accede to my request, the one seated nearest me seized hold of my shoulders; another, at the far end of the trestle bed grasped my feet, and they turned me over upon my stomach as easily as one would a pancake. It certainly occurred to me that I should defend myself, scold them, perhaps even stand and fling myself at them, to fight them, but fever had considerably enfeebled me and besides, given the position in which they had placed me I feared losing dignity. I had mislaid my Amazonian felt hat and my hair, braided into long tresses, must have become undone. Hands like tiny monkeys' paws spread out my locks firmly if not brutally just as they had turned me face downwards. I realised that the women were inspecting my wound. They chattered on and the bed bobbed as one of them rose from it. She fleetingly shut out the light while leaving the hut, and again a moment later when re-entering it. Upon the bruise at the nape of my neck they applied a sort of compress soaked in a liquid which at first caused me a severe, almost red-hot, pain soon succeeded by a delicious sensation of freshness. One of the women burst into bubbling laughter like that of a baby or a bird. I no longer even wanted to turn over again for I felt so relaxed and composed. I all but wondered whether to thank the female savages.

Then, the very instant I entertained this absurd notion, one of the creatures undid the top back buttons of my close-fitting riding habit, tightly tailored as it was from neck to waist, and they undertook to divest me of it. I wished to face them this time, but they merely required to place a knee, a hand, perhaps a fist, upon the small of my back in order to keep me helpless. It was no longer the little wound at the base of my skull but a dreadful shame which overcame me. Button by button, little by little, the creatures rendered me naked as an infant. From time to time they would converse loudly in their pagan lingo. I did not know whether it was I who interested them most or my clothes. These savages were indeed demented. One of them enclosed my posteriors in the palms of her hands and before I could resist had spread my nates as best she could so as to examine me further at her leisure. Perhaps encouraged by this action, another one, at the far end of the bed, in her turn parted my feet and legs, and a third – unless it was she who had desired to inspect my backside – took advantage of this and slid her hand between my thighs. I immediately struggled, forcing my legs violently together and keeping them tight closed. But the strange creatures only laughed. Instead of insisting, being vexed, or perhaps striking me, as I had envisaged (and I was actually contemplating hurling myself upon them and scratching them with my nails), they contented themselves with seizing my feet and shoulders and once again turning me over like a pancake, this time upon my back.

'Oh!' they exclaimed as soon as I was thus exposed.

Oh Wicked Country

At twenty six years of age no one had ever seen me quite naked, at least not since infancy. As I myself said, I used to avoid looking at myself when abluting, and when dressing or undressing. I desperately wanted to curl up, to shelter from all these stares if only by covering my eyes so that I should not see the creatures staring at me. They prevented my doing this, however, by holding me down and by sitting in all simplicity upon my limbs. They began behaving more and more like mad persons. One of them would pull back my eyelids insistently whenever I tried to close them and her enormous black pupils stared fixedly into my blue ones, as if they had been wells into which she might sink. Another grasped hold of my breasts and seemed not to tire of weighing them, encircling them and squeezing them between her fingers. She even went so far as to seize one after the other between her lips and to suck at their tips, which had the immediate effect of making the latter swell and harden; one might have said that the breasts themselves were knotting, hastening my heart's beat. Yet another native, with an entranced air, coiled a finger deep into my navel. She also concluded by introducing her tongue and dawdling therein - which elicited from me a violent shudder. But while I strove to push her off me or in any case to ignore her, the companions of this crazed female, profiting by my inattention, once again spread apart my thighs. One of them knelt between my legs, preventing me from closing them again, then severally, with a prattling chorus of exclamations, they leaned over my sex. Tiny nimble hands ruffled my fleece - doubtless flattened by my clothing and the prolonged ride. Devil take them! I thought. Had they never seen a woman and did they not know how we are made? Indeed, did they not have bodies (for want of the rest) similar to our own?

One of the young creatures - for it was my ill-luck that there seemed none in the company of age or appearance remotely reasonable, let alone, dare I say, respectable - suddenly delivered an even louder cry. She held up one finger in the air and her companions laughed, wrinkling their ridiculous little noses. She who had cried out rushed forth, skipping and gambolling, to return shortly after, bearing with her - rather more carefully - a kind of calabash filled with fresh water and a variety of sponges. Pads made of vegetation or moss, to be precise, like those brought back by travellers from Egypt. The odious creatures then took it upon themselves to wash me. And to be truthful, I who cherish cleanliness would never wish upon any woman the treatment I had then. They used me with less ceremony than one would an animal or even an object such as a nude statue of antiquity, scouring and poking into the smallest folds and hollows of my body, exposing its most intimate secrets with their fingers and their absurd sponges, as if to wipe away not only all traces of a journey, exhaustion and fever, but also the veriest vestige of my own scent, the healthy glow of an English body, and, quite simply, of every civilised human being generally. And while they thus scrubbed me with a slovenliness more illusory than actual, the impression of which was conveyed by their peculiar and crude disportment as savages, a frightful event took place.

I was lying on my back, the creatures having spread my legs wide. They were dabbing at my affair with their little sponges, even venturing so far as to draw the latter to and fro, up and down, along its very lips when at the same time one of them, either to join in the operation or to see the better, put her hand upon my stomach and leaned on it with all her might. To my unspeakable shame, this pressure and the sudden weight reawakened my need so urgently that I passed water despite myself. I had rather been dead at that moment – yet one never does die for a trifle, after all. Whilst all the young women exclaimed more than ever and laughed riotously, I let myself go, urinating for an unconscionable time. I seemed to have turned into a monstrous mare in a field, back home in England. For a brief moment I understood the sheer happiness of being an animal.

'The Devil take these sluts!' I thought, closing my eyes so as not to see them any more.

They had all smartly retreated from the bed in order to escape a wetting. When I had finally done, I wondered without being overly curious, what they intended. Actually I was feeling happy at being an animal, an object. The young creatures were not unduly disconcerted. They behaved towards me as one does to the sick. One of them went out and brought back an armful of dense foliage. When she returned several of her companions raised me while another bundled up the leaves I had soiled and went outside, evidently to dispose of them. The fresh leaves were unfurled and set down in the same place and I was laid back thereon. After which - the incident having hugely diverted them - the young women set to again at my *toilette*, this time concentrating in particular upon my thighs and private parts. When they had laved me thoroughly, they were equally scrupulous to dry me, employing some flaxen stuffs. These were not of course any linens with which we are familiar. The natives weave them themselves from the fibres of that lily-plant botanists call phormium. Lazily, passively, I let myself be handled.

'Busy yourselves, work for me if it amuses you, you silly slaves,' I thought.

I had quite forgotten Frank and England by then. Especially Frank – it was rather as if the situation and these extraordinary events were my revenge upon him as well as on the creatures. Just when I had branded them as slaves, the youngest among them - perhaps fifteen or sixteen years of age, judging by her pointed breasts - asked some question of her companions, who seemed to grant their consent. Whereupon the girl savage – I gathered her name was Nawa-Na - sat with all the snakelike suppleness of the natives on the edge of the bed and, turning to face me began tapping upon the trestle nearest her. I watched her without moving. Then the others, still without cruelty, but also without the slightest hesitation, laid hold of my shoulders and forced me upright, compelling me to sit beside the creature.

Her slanting brown eyes smiled but not her lips. I was completely naked while she wore what was apparently the regulation issue white loincloth of this tribe - so I was placed in a humiliating position. On the other hand, although I am not particularly tall, I seemed to tower over the young creature even though we were seated; from my head with its fair hair, to my shoulders and whole body, my proudly blooming bosom, I was built on a larger scale than she. Frank, I recalled, had never liked nor appreciated my breasts. The young girl Nawa-Na took one of them in her hand and gently weighed it for a moment. Yet that was not what truly interested her. I did not understand why, but what decidedly took her fancy was that blonde downy fur upon my parts, even though it was far less prominent now I was seated. She leaned across in order to look more closely at it and her hand and fingers momentarily toyed with it. I myself was overcome with amazement.

Then the other women said a few words to Nawa-Na and she ceased her inspection, took hold of the top of my arm and drew me towards her. Understanding even less than before, I resisted, but the other women approached with what seemed a menacing air and I had to yield. What Nawa-Na wanted was for me to lie face downwards across her, resting on her knees. This new position horrified me, for thus I was exposed, naked, and quite unable to keep watch on the women who were looking at me. But to my shame and my rage too the very last straw was this: the young girl, after disposing me to her liking, with my haunches elevated over her own thighs, simply set to and began spanking me as we might chastise a disobedient child at home.

Oh Wicked Country

For some reason my parents never beat me, and so this was the first time I, aged twenty-six, had ever received a spanking. My self-respect was absolutely outraged and I was especially vexed by the idea of getting beaten before the very eyes of these creatures, and at the hands, furthermore, of someone who in my own eyes was no more than a wretched slip of a girl. As soon as I tried to turn and raise myself up however, she would press her free hand between my shoulder-blades and I realised that the other women would come to her aid were I to persist. I was therefore obliged to submit and to continue to allow myself to be scourged. The wild urchin went at it with all her might and main. The smarting sensation was such that sometimes I would contract despite myself, to escape it, and sometimes (because when I did contract the blows and slaps upon the taut muscles caused me such acute pain) I would do the reverse and relax, lie limp and open, forcing myself to be as limber as possible and hence, ironically, invulnerable. But then that tiny furious palm would strike me straight on the anus and on the sexual orifice – which seemed to be gaping open with a strange sort of hunger exacerbated and provoked by the burning sensation – and I could not long endure it. Still the beating continued and my anger and rebellious pride reached breaking-point. Once past that point, since the blows rained down, seemingly redoubled in both quantity and weight, something in my spirit broke and I started to weep and then burst out sobbing, struggling bitterly the while. The women screamed with satisfaction.

While I was kicking and fighting – though I must confess without really trying to get up, nor to protect myself from the blows – I chanced to turn my head towards the great door of the hut and there, a few yards away, I saw a native pass. It was a man, naked save for the loincloth. Perhaps because of the noise he slowed pace and himself turned towards the hut. I was certain that he saw me also, more naked than himself, and being spanked like a child; I thought he might approach and enter the hut. At this idea, as if torn from the very depths of my womb, there came a fierce, rending convulsion, flooding me with savage pleasure. Suddenly everything, deep within my sex, seemed to burn and melt. The man had in fact scarcely paused in his stride and had gone off, but the creatures, with their diabolic instincts did not fail to remark the exact moment of my unthinkable reaction. They exclaimed anew with joy, clapped their hands, and thronged round me and their companion.

Nawa-Na beat me for a few seconds more but with less fervour. One might have considered it more akin to calming me, an appeasement of sorts. She ceased, and I remained supine over her knees, my bottom spread, blazing and no doubt bright scarlet. Taking advantage of my abandonment the young girl sank not only one finger but it seemed her whole tiny hand into my quim, withdrew it and repeated the process a few times rather charmingly. She laughed, and I gathered that she was explaining to her companions that I was vanquished and that the access of pleasure had soaked me, flooding with juice my vitals. Yet neither her laughter nor my defeat succeeded in humiliating me. Quite the contrary; my pride was once again restored, immense, and it sailed above those miserable creatures like an eagle. When Nawa-Na decided at last to withdraw her hand entirely, I should have liked to take it in mine and to kiss each finger.

When they left the hut the women had taken away my clothing. I thought that this was a means of keeping me captive. It was possible that they merely wished to try on the clothes and play at dressing up. Perhaps they too had husbands, native brown-skinned Franks – an idea which struck me as ineffably comical – and themselves sought to make use of my wardrobe in order to seduce them! I remained lying upon my stomach, feeling under me the springy mattress of leaves, and indifferent to everything. My hurdies still stung. I was no longer in pain, nor did I even consider the bruise upon my nape. A dull sensation like giddiness persisted, curiously, in my womb and each time my thoughts turned, despite themselves, to dwell upon this secretly kindled flame, my nipples hardened. I listlessly ran my fingers through the dense foliage on which I lay.

Much later I grew hungry and thirsty. I did not want to give the natives any importance, but the noises of their activities reached me. The men, hitherto absent or unseen, with the sole exception of the one I had seen while being spanked, seemed to return to the village in the evening. Women greeted each other, pounding heaven knows what roots in mortars or crushing them upon stone or wooden trays. I heard children laughing and

running about. Of course the savages themselves
were but children too. Perhaps I should have called
out or tried to escape but, to be truthful, I think not.
I was hungry and thirsty, but otherwise I was not
suffering, that was all one could say. I believe I
slept. When I opened my eyes it felt colder. I also
had the impression that the slight rain, thereabouts
well-nigh perpetual, had stopped, and through the
gaps between the battens and the greenery of the hut
walls I perceived that they had lit a large fire. At
length I turned over again upon my back, then sat
up, my back resting against the partition wall made
up of woven leafage. I felt very isolated, albeit too
listless or bewildered to be afraid.

Shortly afterwards, the doorway panel was pulled
aside and a group of women entered. Nawa-Na was
not among them; I recognised only one or two faces.
It seemed that all the others were newcomers.
Through the aperture behind the women I indeed
discerned an enormous pyramidal bonfire, with
women, children and men seated round about it,
eating and gossiping among themselves. One of the
women who had just entered bore my clothes over
one arm. I noted at once that these had been washed.
A second held in both hands a basin of clean water
and, threaded into a necklace, the same small
sponges of vegetable matter. Yet another addressed
me, which was ridiculous, for I could not understand her. As I did not reply, she leaned across
and pressed my loins with one hand, looking at me
meaningfully as she did so. I supposed that she was
asking whether I wished to relieve myself again, and
I indicated that I did. Thereupon she removed

another panel from the wall opposite the main opening and took me through it, several yards further into the darkness, amidst very dense undergrowth of bushes and trees. I squatted and swiftly relieved myself. This made the young woman laugh. In the bright starlight I could see her face, and when I stood up, I could not help looking at her questioningly in my turn. She laughed anew, then in a trice doffed her loincloth and showed me how she herself conducted matters. Native women in fact remain almost upright for the purpose, slightly bending their knees. It was unseemly, and the noise in particular well and truly unbearable. I had a sudden very lively desire to catch sight of her parts while she made water, but unfortunately the light did not extend so far and only illumined her face, leaving almost all her body in shadow. I had the impression that she dried herself promptly with a handful of leaves before rewinding her loincloth.

Inside the hut they bade me stand up, my legs half-open while they washed me once more, though in more perfunctory fashion, around the loins, inner thighs and beneath the arms too. After which the women attired me from top to toe, with the exception however of stockings, which they denied me. It took them several attempts and I had to assist them. They would confuse the sleeves and other openings of a garment, or were baffled by buttons, ribbons and hooks. When I was at last dressed they allowed me to sit upon the bed, and other women brought me victuals and drink. The water was very fresh and the meal of fish, coarsely prepared though it was, seemed delicious to me. While eating – and especially drinking – I wondered if such treatment would continue as long as I remained in these savages' power: that they would wait upon me, feed me, dress and undress me in this same hut, all without ever allowing me the right to leave it other than furtively to satisfy a need, after dusk and on condition that I turned my back (in a manner of speaking) upon the village.

I was mistaken however. While I ate the women waited without impatience, talking amongst themselves in lower tones though with far less laughter than on the preceding afternoon. As soon as I had finished they gave me to understand that I was to rise and follow them forthwith. I obeyed, vaguely gratified to find myself taller than any of their number.

The moment I crossed the threshold of the hut it seemed as if the very world itself loomed around me. There was the immense night sky with stars different from those we in England know, and below it a circle or semi-circle of mountains, whose proud peaks I distinguished in the distance – though by contrast some of them looked plain and even threadbare silhouetted against the heavens. Within that outer ring, so to speak, lay a more gradually sloping inner ring of hills, their dense burden of trees giving them almost a fleecy appearance. Then at the centre, in space more or less scooped out of trees and bush, the natives had built and arranged their dwellings and huts. The collective term in Maori is *pah*, though naturally I did not then know it. At the very centre of the *pah*, or village if you prefer, I saw only the confused, anonymous mass of natives huddled together, crouching or kneeling around the fire for the evening meal. There was no one near the hut wherein I had been held captive, and it was from this deserted side of the *pah* that the women led me into their midst. Having done so, they too went to sit amid the throng.

The firelight fitfully lit the naked bodies of the savages. I was quite alone there, standing motionless between the fire and the people staring at me. Only some children stood, as I did, and they were running hither and thither. To maintain my dignity and composure I myself affected not to look at or see anyone. It seemed there were speculations and discussions well under way, but these were muted and without much merriment. I began to hope that when their curiosity was satisfied they would respect my status as an Englishwoman or even a White European, perhaps with a view to an exchange of hostages or some form of bargaining, and that I would be led back to the hut. But there was no sign of that either.

A command was given. From the corner of my eye I had discerned a man who, judging by his stature even while seated, was very likely the chief. I eventually came to know him as Ra-Hau. But that night he did not appear to exercise any authority. Then two women stood up, approached me and without more ado began undressing me.

'It was scarcely worth the trouble,' I thought to myself.

I all but laughed with rage. They stripped me naked save for my nether garments - a flimsy set of drawers in the English mode, trimmed with silk, lawn and lacework - which concealed the indecorous areas of the body from waist to thigh. I still felt relief at having got off so lightly.

The women had me turn about so that everyone might readily see me. Such a movement momentarily made my naked bosom swing and my long blonde hair fanned out between my shoulders. A deep throaty murmuring issued from the menfolk. A boy sprang from the crowd, ran towards me and hurled himself at me. He gripped the tops of my thighs with all his might, and since it happened that his face was just level with my stomach, he bent his head and ardently thrust his lips upon my sex, through my garment. The material was so fine that I felt the warmth and even the shape of his mouth, as he must have done, though with my most intimate being. I was so surprised that I could not cuff him nor push him away. He nuzzled at me for a moment, giving me a still more urgent and insistent kiss, then ran off, his action eliciting no more than a renewed murmur, which, it seemed to me, in no way betokened disapprobation. I was half dead with shame, the more so because this urchin, like all the other youths (and their elders too, of course) wore the classic loincloth. I do not know why I should have preferred the children at least to go naked. I think I might have felt less alone.

Someone clapped his hands. There then appeared a species of wooden horse somewhat similar to those which gymnasts in England use, although this one was upholstered with foliage instead of leather, and they arranged the contrivance parallel to the crowd. It was lower than a vaulting-horse, and like the impudent urchin, was almost of a height with my stomach. While I was examining it with astonishment rather than disquiet, for even nightmares are themselves but variants of dream, the pair of women who had undressed me, suddenly seized me. They laid me across the curious apparatus and left me there, just like a captive one flings, trussed, over the saddle of a horse. I was thus disposed face downwards, my head and torso on the side of the fire, my legs and hindquarters - those beastly feminine regions! - turned to the crowd, which little by little had thronged together to form a block rather than a circle.

I was not tied, yet I dared not so much as stir, or offer the least resistance, fearing perpetually that my captors might do me far worse injury. It was horrid enough to know and know so ignominiously that I was exposing to those lewd stares the precise configuration of my body and especially of my haunches, still parted owing to that unseemly position into which I had been placed. And as I attempted to make myself smaller, to contract as best I could, so as to escape their greedy perusal of me, someone again clapped. I might just as well have spared myself the effort.

One of the two women who had just placed me on the horse and whom I recognised, when I turned my head - very slightly in order not to risk altering position - came back, slid behind me (and I was intensely aware of her presence there, as if I could actually feel her in my very marrow) and without warning placed her hands upon my hips and pulled my drawers down to my knees. Everyone present uttered a guttural exclamation. Overwhelmed by shame, I felt myself blush, and not only upon the cheeks or the whole face but over my entire body from head to toe. It was so insufferable that I should have liked to close my eyes never to reopen them, yet at the same time I could not even for a moment lose sight of those who were engaged in staring at me.

I do not know why, but it seems that in the most humiliating situation one can preserve a modicum of pride, as long as one strives to be somewhat detached and to stare back defiantly at those observing oneself. In my profoundest shame, with everything that is most secret, hidden and intimate in the womanly body thus displayed and set on show for the eyes of spectators, I never refrained from turning my head from side to side in order to survey these spectators and be apprised of their possible approach. Certain of them had indeed risen to their feet and one man walked towards the horse. It was my misfortune to lose sight of him, of necessity, at the very moment he was closest me – behind me, that is – when I should most have wished to monitor his every move.

Yet I could merely sense and suffer what he was to do. Before he was out of my field of vision I had seen only that this was not the tall, strong-looking native I adjudged to be the chief. This was just an ordinary individual much like the rest, and I hated him all the more on this account. It seemed to me that my degradation would have been less profound had it been the work of a chief. Determining that I had closed my legs so as to hide myself, he must have bent down, for he seized my ankles and pulled them apart again. The delicate hem of my drawers was tightly stretched around my knees but did not give way. The man then spread open my posteriors with the palms of his hands, at the same time ensuring with his thumbs that my sexual aperture too was agape. Bent almost double and parted so from behind, a woman is absolutely defenceless, there is nothing she can do. I seemed to feel the spectators' very breath upon the interior of my body - laid bare as it then was - and I thought I heard them whisper and gasp. The man who was exploring and exposing me said something in jest, and it also seemed to me that the others were bantering with him as they gradually moved back.

Then he suddenly plunged a finger inside my sex. Brutally, I may say, for the pleasure I had experienced that afternoon had long since vanished, and now, a prey to the shame and anger prompted by all those stares, I felt cold, dry, and so narrowly contracted that the man had in fact to force me, well-nigh violate me in a sense, while doing no more than sink a single finger into me. In doing so he hurt me greatly and I detested him more than ever. Then he slowly removed the finger, saying something or other to the surrounding crowd, his tone of voice betraying evident dissatisfaction. While he was withdrawing it however, I felt the walls of my sex cleave to the finger despite myself, as if trying to hold it there in some grotesque parody of desire and love. One of the natives again clapped his hands, pronouncing in authoritative tones a name or a brief command:

'Ga-Wau! Ga-Wau!'

Oh Wicked Country

I started trembling with fear, assuming they were about to punish me and inflict some dreadful revenge upon me for not having shown myself, at the first entreaty, to be complaisant, warm and willing like a real woman. To all appearances at least I had been, on the contrary, numb and unresponsive. A different set of footsteps approached the horse-contrivance; these were light and nimble. Twisting my head a little I recognised the lad who had embraced me when I had been undressed. He also moved behind me and suddenly, just as I realised who he was, I felt once more the contact of his lips – this time directly upon the entrance and, one might almost say, the interior, of my sex. His warm muzzle was wholly pressed into the area between my thighs and buttocks and on either side I also felt the brushing and tickling sensation from his hair. He was not content to press kisses as strongly and as hard as he could but had succeeded, I realised, in actually penetrating me with his tongue. I am certain that at any other time I could not have deferred my crisis. I would have flooded the greedy little mouth and the hot little tongue, lively, rasping yet soft as it was, with all the juices of my ecstasy. But to tell the truth I was too much on edge, too icy despite the burning shame, or perhaps because of it. The boy Ga-Wau in his turn regretfully withdrew his tongue and tender muzzle and departed, or rejoined the crowd. The same commanding voice, even harsher if anything, called out a name I recognised:

'Nawa-Na!'

I shuddered, distraught. I thought she was going

to give me another thrashing. I could not bear the idea of this happening in front of not just a few young women but before men and children too, and in the presence of aged folk and the tribal elders – indeed, before the entire community. Yet at the same time the fact that I already knew the girl and she had previously witnessed my utter abandonment, somehow reassured me and even brought an absurd, comforting glow to my whole being. She had already beaten me and, rightly or wrongly, whatever one experiences – albeit only once – lessens subsequent apprehension. Snatching a glance as best I could to one side of the horse, I espied the slender brown legs of her whom, in my inmost depths (and this was doubtless ridiculous), I considered as a sort of friend. However, from what I could see, she was wearing not only a loincloth but had also wrapped a fold of material around her bosom, supporting and concealing her breasts, as if she too deemed it her duty to make me feel more naked, more exposed, still more wretched. When she was behind me she too bent over, and finally removed my drawers, which like a purely symbolic last bastion had remained about my knees, and taking me by the shoulders, made me stand up. As I turned towards her I also turned towards the crowd and their exclamations were again audible. There was no need to wonder why.

Nawa-Na, observing those who had exclaimed, seemed to answer them, smiling as she raised an eyebrow, then momentarily took a sort of one-handed bowling grip upon the exposed part of my sex and its blonde fur. After which she faced me

again. As we stood there together, it was clear that
Nawa-Na was not only much younger but much
smaller and slimmer than I. Her smile seemed
bemused and preoccupied rather than mocking. As
for me, who, like any sensible person, abhors
natives, I surprised myself – in this nightmarish
situation – by sincerely admiring this young girl's
huge dark eyes; her thick and flowing ebony-hued
hair; her tiny nose, slightly flattened so that her
nostrils flared like corollae; her dazzling white teeth
and her full, beautiful lips.

Between the vaulting-horse (which I eventually
discovered to be a frame more customarily used for
smoking and drying fish) and the hut where I had
been kept, the grass-covered terrain formed a sort of
bench or shallow step several yards long, tilted as
though intentionally towards the small crowd of
natives. Nawa-Na went to sit upon this natural
bench, thus facing her peers and intimated with a
nod that I should rejoin her. When one is naked one
wishes to move about as little as possible, for the
least change of position uncovers and reveals yet
more. But I knew full well I had no choice and I
complied.

'Not in front of them, not in front of all these
people!' I thought despairingly.

As in a nightmare, however, the scene of the
afternoon repeated itself. Nawa-Na led me to
understand that I was to lie face down across her
knees, and there too I was obliged to obey. The girl
even turned slightly to one side so that my buttocks
were fully visible to each of the onlookers.

'Let her beat me if she will, she shan't make me

weaken or soften, she'll only manage to make me colder still,' I thought, with the same despairing fury.

But this time Nawa-Na had not the intention of spanking me or in any case not in the way she had done that afternoon. No doubt she knew quite as well as I that that would not have sufficed. The little slut, even while she had been depriving me of my drawers and making me get up and then setting me over her knees must have been concealing – whether by hiding it in the grass or holding it treacherously behind her back – a dildo. With this thin and very flexible stave she promptly started beating my backside. The surprise, quite as much as the pain, was so pronounced and keen that I had not time to summon my resolution or my courage, and I immediately began shrieking, sobbing and struggling. Just as she had during the afternoon, Nawa-Na simply struck me all the harder; she contented herself with taking fiendish pains not to beat my loins and thighs, and confined her attentions exclusively to my rump. On this occasion however it seemed as if every blow were lacerating me.

I had lost all shame and modesty and was yelling like a madwoman, sobbing and begging her to desist. While I was struggling I did manage to slide my legs off the bench, if not off the girl's knees. She, with the strength the savages have – apparently even the frailest among them – grasped me forcibly beneath her left arm, imprisoning me by my waist, and spanked me still more energetically and in far more hurtful manner, for this new position, with my own knees almost touching the grass, meant that my bottom jutted out more prominently, its cheeks still more vulnerably parted. I confess that while Nawa-Na redoubled her onslaught I thought the stave would literally tear me open. And not only my haunches and skin at that, but the approaches to, and unspeakably delicate membranes of, my fundament and sex. Yet even as I experienced this fear, the burning and tearing sensation itself seemed to delve into my very depths, bursting I know not what dams, so that while gripped by the utmost pain I could feel the sap of pleasure spill from my inner recesses, gathering momentum like a cataract. With her uncanny instinct, Nawa-Na immediately guessed as much and, at once stopped beating me. She drew me up with her, apparently effortlessly, as if her slender grace hid muscles of steel, and led me back vanquished and sobbing to the horse-cum-frame, upon which they positioned me once again.

I no longer dreamed of defending myself; I was like a bundle of dirty linen. I was sure that the trail of my pleasure must have been distinctly visible between my thighs, yet despite this I had not the strength to close my legs nor even to remain long thus, arched over the leaves with my buttocks wide open and my sex in full view. Anyhow they did not leave me alone for long. While I continued weeping bitterly, my cheek pressed against the foliage, and hiding (from myself rather than from the others) behind my long tresses and my tears, a man, probably the same one who had inserted his finger into me, came up behind me once more. I only caught a glimpse of his sinewy legs, which were rather short like those of most natives, especially the men's. He lingered only long enough no doubt to unwind his loincloth, then with one hand (somewhat unnecessarily under the circumstances) spread the lips of my sex and with the other placed against its opening – as Frank used to do, but without Frank's horrid gropings – his own swollen member. With one thrust of his loins he then sank the entire object deep inside me.

It is said that men always complain of what they find in women. Before my beating I had sensed that this man, when penetrating me digitally had been disappointed to the verge of irritation by the tightness and dryness of my sex. I had the impression that he was just as discontented now, when it was prepared, thoroughly softened and anointed by the fluids of pleasure. He would have preferred to violate me with his weapon as he had done with his finger. Perhaps men always seek something other than what they already have. My aggressor must also have been displeased by the scant enjoyment he gave me. He ought to have understood that he was in fact too late.

In spite of myself I had taken my pleasure, an awful pleasure but as overwhelming as a cataclysm, under the last beating from Nawa-Na, and after such an upheaval the sturdiest man could only have been no more than a casual, indifferent guest between my thighs and within my vagina. It was, so to speak, as if he soaked himself inside me, profiting by my moistness and heat, but his own individual qualities did not touch me. I noticed only that his member was both a little shorter and thicker than Frank's. He slightly distended the outer ring of my vagina when his organ passed through it, and that was very nearly all I felt. Neither the penetration of the whole shaft, nor its to-and-fro motions – somewhat brief in any case – nor finally the sort of absurd sneeze inside me, embellished with a male groan both shaken and frustrated, moved me to any degree.

I was expecting all the other tribesmen to violate me, after this one, and I had resigned myself to it. After what I had endured so far, all else left me indifferent. But that was not to be either. As I still lay draped over the frame some young girls staunched my parts with crushed herbs, raised me to my feet, and also wiped my abdomen and the pubic area in the same manner before leading me back to the hut, where I remained alone. I was an object they had used, and which is afterwards cast aside. Male voices were chanting rhythmically outside, around the fire. The laughter and lighter voices of the women provided a confused kind of music by way of counterpoint.

I supposed that it was when I awoke the next morning that I truly began to suffer from my abandonment among the savages and from loneliness. Although it may seem perfectly dreadful to admit it, for as long as they tormented and beat me, as long as they penetrated and violated me, they were in a peculiar way recognising and thus affirming my existence. They and their tortures afforded me points of reference, society of sorts.

For several days thereafter they denied me that society and consequently, a sense of my existence. I was no longer even an object, or so it seemed to me. Nothing but the abstract, artificial and quite arbitrary recollection of an alleged previous life, elsewhere, in a place I called England, with people called Frank, Colonel Percy Smyth, Sir John and Lady McLeod, and the like. One does not, however, live upon recollections. They take life from us, that is all.

At seemingly irregular intervals, some women and young girls would enter the hut, wash me, and bring me food and drink, more or less keeping to the ritual of dressing me from head to toe in the morning and undressing me completely at night. They were in the habit of gossiping amongst themselves or of smiling vaguely at me. Then that stopped. Whether it was due to a refinement of cruelty or to sheer indifference, I had no longer even the petty satisfaction of relief at seeing one of these faces to which I could put a name: Ga-Wau, the little boy with the inquisitive, merry eyes; athletic Ra-Hau, or sly Nawa-Na with her dildoes. Sometimes one or another anonymous tribesman would enter. He would give me a brief dispassionate glance, he too would exchange a few words with whichever women were there, and would then go away again, vanishing, leaving me to my limbo of nothingness.

One day, exasperated by this terrifying sense of uselessness, I resolved to stroll on my own account through the village. It was mid-afternoon and I found myself quite alone. I made certain that my apparel – dress, linen, shoes and even the shawl I once used to wear as a riding-cloak – was absolutely clean and neat, then without further ado I slid aside the panel of foliage. I emerged into bright sunshine; the day was still misted with fine rain and the world looked beautiful. I recognised the large grassy central area and the burnt-out fire near which the beating and fornication had taken place. At the edge of this clearing there grew luxuriant vegetation, verdant, thick and shiny, dominated by giant conifers – *kauris* – amid which more huts were scattered. These trees covered the hillsides. Further off still, lay a bluish ring of mountains whose outlines were crisply etched against the sky, sometimes almost perfectly conical, their summits dazzlingly snowcapped. But here in the natural bowl where the *pah*, the village, was situated, the temperature was mild, gently humid and warm. I thought, however, that I detected a hidden, bracing freshness which suggested the presence of running water or of a deep clear lake nearby.

No one prevented me from issuing forth, nor forbade my promenade. And yet it was a heart-rending experience. The bitterest thing for me to accept was that the duration of the stroll, the life of the natives and their village went on, but went on without me. Children played. For the first time I met some who were completely naked. They were having a sort of siesta, lying upon the grass. I found myself stirred, and I felt my womb contract momentarily, without my knowing why. Perhaps it was because for the first time I was dressed, they naked. Or simply that their skins, their pale brown bodies were so pretty. Flawless, spotless. I had an almost irresistible urge to caress these children, boys and girls alike, to fill my palms with their charming little bottoms, to sink my lips for refreshment between their rounded haunches and to take in my mouth and suck like fruits the tiny, oddly swollen vulvas of the girls and the miniature penises of the boys. Naturally I refrained from so doing, and they, the children, paid me no more attention than their elders did.

For their part the women relaxed also, as carefree as the children, or were carding phormium leaves with bone and wooden combs, carrying water, or busying themselves with cooking or storing food-stuffs. Some of them were enjoying themselves and playfully wrestling with each other. That day there were men in the village. Like the women, they too were conversing and entertaining themselves, or else were occupied with sharpening weapons, fashioning arrowheads, restoring the leafy walls of huts, and sometimes plucking one of those birds so plentiful in New Zealand (mammals are almost unknown there). These birds are roasted whole over the fire, within a form of thin pastry, or cooked deliciously beneath heated stones, inside a jacket of clay.

Yet neither men nor women, boys nor girls, showed any interest in me whatever. Eyes would be raised when I passed, or someone might go as far as to smile absently; some, the women especially, would give my clothing a cursory glance, then each would resume their activities. I might as well have been but a trick of the light or the merest atmospheric change. Apparently there was not the least concern that I might attempt to escape, and this was perhaps more humiliating, depressing and cruel than all else.

I walked to the outskirts of the *pah* and wandered for a long time through huge ferns and trees. No one followed me nor thought to do so. For a while I felt that I would have flung myself at the feet of the first creature I encountered – were they male or female, it little mattered – and begged: 'Beat me, rape me, flay me – only pray don't leave me upon my own!'

I met no one whose glance returned mine long enough for me to convey my supplication. Anyway no one would have understood, for the savages found my language as incomprehensible as I did the Maori tongue. Therefore I could address nobody and say nothing. Despite myself, I suddenly fell to weeping, and ran back to my wretched 'home' without evoking any response, not even curiosity, concerning the motive for my absence.

I sometimes thought I was going mad. But one never does go mad; I am no longer sure why not. One is mad and does not know it. On one or another of those days the women entered my hut at a time when I was usually left alone. I was lying fully-clothed upon the bed, whose leafage was daily renewed, just as I was partly or wholly washed, almost at every visit, and I was growing bored. My heart beat faster when among the women and girls I recognised Nawa-Na. Out of modesty, I hid my

44

emotions and she in her turn smiled at me with her customary artlessness, as if she had been the one to harbour no hard feelings towards myself. The other women made way for her. She came across to me, slipped a hand under my arm, and indicated that I should turn over, face downwards. All this was by now familiar to me, and I obeyed, my heart pounding with distress and also a sort of delirious impatience. But the young woman did not strike me.

She pulled my long skirts past my haunches, pulled down my drawers, spread my posteriors and suddenly pressed an adorable kiss into the hollow of my fugo. Then she burst into that cool clear laughter of hers. I was trembling with fear and tenderness. The other women helped Nawa-Na strip me naked as the day I was born. As soon as I had not a stitch on, the women, for once deeming me clean enough, led me out of the hut. Only one of them, though, as soon as we had crossed the threshold, assured herself by grimacing and pressing upon my stomach, that I was in absolutely no need of emptying my bladder. The insistence and oddity of such questions made me blush inexplicably, just as being led naked by savages amid other savages could do nothing but hasten the already excitable beatings of my heart in a manner scarcely supportable.

For once it was not raining outside. The sun was fierce and though heavy and stickily sweet as honey, it beat like a vast golden hand against my nakedness. I saw too that in the village there were many more natives than on my previous excursion, and that their interest was aroused. I admit that that made me shudder. They were observing me deliberately, it seemed to me, concentrating their attention upon my female aperture, ill-concealed beneath its fleece. Nawa-Na gently took my hand and began running. I was horrified to run naked, to denude myself as it were still further by such motion, my breasts and flanks in an indecent dance before the eyes of all. Yet in another sense, this rapid movement itself concealed and somewhat spared me. Nawa-Na was tugging me along towards that frightful vaulting-horse, and when I realised this I could not help but slow my stride and resist. But she dragged me all the more firmly, turning her head to smile at me over her shoulder.

'No, no!' I protested silently. Deaf to such entreaties, she placed me as before across the infernal contrivance, head on one side, legs upon the other, my buttocks exposed and vulnerable. How I began trembling again when I heard a large number of the tribe approach and surround us! Nawa-Na bade me rise. She held a discussion with the other women and certain onlookers. I understood that they did not want to leave me exposed to the full heat of the sun, because the sun might alter the hue of my skin, and it was precisely my pallor which entertained the natives and excited them by its novelty. Perhaps my position simply did not appeal to them. They led me back, indeed, to the edge of the clearing, which in some way served as the assembly site and main square of the village, and there, while I stood waiting, in the cooler shade which the giant ferns and trees cast over the grass, a handful of natives hurriedly erected a second contrivance. The latter vaguely resembled a bed, only slightly higher off the ground than their usual couches, and bore a slight resemblance to the vaulting-horse in that it has a pronounced convexity at its centre: a hump-backed bed, if you will. Of course I was ignorant of its exact purpose, but was in no doubt that it concerned myself. Accordingly I took the desperate decision not to wait this time until they should compel me; immediately the natives had strewn fresh leaves over it I lay face down of my own free will, my body also arched with my flanks prominent owing to the shape of the mattress. At least, I thought to myself, that would conceal my breasts and sex.

Yet this spontaneous gesture of obedience drew wild laughter not only from Nawa-Na but from most of those present, the women in particular. What they wanted was precisely the opposite – that I should lie upon my back, and they speedily saw to it that I turned over again. At that I felt truly appalled because my entire nether parts and sex were now higher than my head, exhibited for everyone's delectation. What added to the horror of such a position was this: with my head and feet now positioned lower than the exposed parts, it was impossible for me to see, or in some measure protect, this sensitive area. On the other hand, I could now see all too well – as I could not when I had been placed upon the vaulting-horse – every one of the natives who surrounded me as each drew near and leaned over to examine and jabber about the parted lips and exposed orifice (more naked than nudity itself) of my sex, the sex which I myself could no longer see. To see less of myself than others can see: I consider the fiendish savages expert in such refinements.

Then they spread my arms and legs. I understood that they were debating whether to bind them to the four corners of the makeshift bed. But Nawa-Na shrugged her shoulders laughingly. For a long time she at least had had no doubts as to my obedience, or rather resignation. She requested those who had taken hold of me to let me go, quite certain that I was not going to move, and contented herself to signalling to several of her companions that they should sit on the edges of the bed, preferably beside my wrists and ankles in case, voluntarily or involuntarily, I did happen to make any movement.

Then she rose to her feet and I lost sight of her as she went away. She returned a moment or so later, bearing with her all kinds of tiny objects. She clambered upon the bottom of the bed, knelt there, and then I again lost sight of her, or rather could only glimpse her brown head, satin shoulders and pretty, pointed breasts when she sat up straight. She herself must have been stretched out upon her stomach, her torso just between my thighs.

Before beginning, she gave the nearest men a half-playful half-mocking order, and they, laughing themselves and blithely shrugging their shoulders, drew back, as always when she was torturing me, so as to give her plenty of room. Certain of them, feigning regret, even resumed their previous occupations. Just as I saw them go off, one of Nawa-Na's hands pinched my vulva, whilst with the other she pressed against my abdomen a small, hard, cold object. I knew by the end that this was in fact a shell, more likely a species of bivalve. But then I felt a sudden pang, both keen and very fleeting. I started, crying out uncontrollably, and instinctively wanted to contract, but at once the women gripped my ankles and wrists, forcing me to remain spread-eagled.

I could not understand what Nawa-Na intended to do. Just before I cried out she had uttered a short, silvery chuckle which attested to her satisfaction. Once again her supple, sinewy fingers pinched my vulva, once again I felt the chill contact of the shell, and once again that sharp red-hot prickling. This time I understood.

With their diabolical intuition the natives had realised that there invariably exists a way of being more naked than one already is. Nawa-Na was engaged in depilating me. Wisp by wisp, hair by hair, she was removing from me, since I was no longer a young maid, what had been – until I fell among savages and was deprived of all clothing and perhaps of every mask of civilisation – in some respects my very last garment. Nature herself had given it me, and it was being taken from me again by these wild children. All in all, the physical pain was quite tolerable, more of a smarting irritation like that produced by swift and repeated pricks from a hairpin, except perhaps when the depilation process, having laid bare all the pubis, gradually neared the groove of the thighs, then the very lips of my sex. And then the women compelled me to raise my knees and forced them back upon my bosom so that Nawa-Na managed to extirpate even the most delicate down remaining on my buttocks and around the anus.

What was impossible for me to bear was the impression of being stripped and despoiled, of mutilation and irreparable loss. This last sensation hurt me more than the loss of my virginity had ever done. After all, virginity is almost entirely a moral restraint, whereas now I was naked for the first time and perhaps nothing would ever clothe me again. I was naked in the eyes of others, but all the more so in my own. Also, during the course of the proceedings (and not at all because of the physical pain, although as I have said, that was intermittently intense), I burst into tears and could not stop until they had ended.

When I was well and truly naked as an earthworm, Nawa-Na, still smiling, sat back on her heels, between my thighs, and with a graceful gesture mopped her brow with the back of her hand as if she had reached the end of some arduous toil. I wept scalding tears, and when she sprang off the bed she let me close my legs and even cover myself with one hand.

I wished the earth could have swallowed me up. I did not know why they did not also remove the hair from my armpits, where I sport merely a tiny wisp of fair hair, in my opinion charming rather than conspicuous or unsightly. Or rather, now that I have learned what the natives are like, I suspect that the object of this omission was to emphasise by contrast, the shocking and aggressive nudity of my lower abdomen and of my vulva itself. I found my depilated motte a monstrous provocation to all and sundry and, as I have said, to myself also. I realised that with every step I took henceforth I would be aware of touching and in some sense caressing my sex's nakedness with my own thighs, and that this contact and awareness would almost make me falter. Merely to imagine it brought on a spasm of voluptuous pleasure which would wrench at my cervix and make me moist inside.

As the operation had probably irritated (in a strictly medical sense) the flesh and very tender membranes nearest the sexual and rectal sphincters, Nawa-Na's companions pushed away my hand and anointed me and massaged me very gently with a healing vegetable balm. I prayed to myself that they would confuse this concoction with the insidious sexual liquid I had released. I continued to weep; I was heartbroken.

At last Nawa-Na lifted me up, took my hand again gently, scolded various men who wished to approach (which again prompted their laughter), and led me back to my hut where she left me. But she and one or two companions bivouacked nearby, doubtless in front of the door. A number of times during the night I heard men's footsteps lingering outside as if they had designs on entry. The men would come alone or in groups of two or three. Nawa-Na's firm, clear little voice, curt yet bantering, reprimanded them and exhorted them to go back to bed. I would fall asleep again myself from pure exhaustion, tired out with weeping.

The following morning I did not see Nawa-Na. She

too must have gone to rest in one of the huts. The other women came, as was their wont, bringing me sustenance, and saw to it that I relieved myself and was washed. They carefully inspected my depilated areas and I, as in England, refused to examine myself. Revealing signs of annoyance, they bathed and massaged my pubis, vulva and inner thighs scrupulously, as on the previous evening. At the mere touch of their palms, I could feel that I was now smooth and soft as an infant. This feeling disgusted me, not in a physical manner, but as if, for example, I had been guilty of some wickedness, and at the same time it disturbed me. Then the women, instead of dressing me, left me naked upon the bed. When they had departed I was unable, despite all, to sit up and look at myself for long. The sight of my denuded, hairless abdomen and especially my sex – that swelling, that prominence with its fleshy folds and tea-rose hue, cleft slyly like a fruit, a huge fig bursting with juice and sugar in the sun – in the very centre of my pale body, the sight of this ineradicable feminine stigma only emphasised my sensations of grief and shame the more bitterly. Though they had refrained from dressing me, the native women had nonetheless returned, as they did every morning, a complete freshly laundered set of my clothes. In order to conceal my shame I risked disobedience, and without looking at myself any more, indeed forcing distractions upon myself such as staring at the palms and foliage which comprised the hut's roof, I hastily donned clean drawers before retiring to bed again.

The moment I lay down Nawa-Na re-entered. I

need hardly add that the first thing she noticed was precisely that I was wearing this undergarment. It made her laugh. She sat sideways upon the bed and immediately leaned over me and removed the drawers, first pulling the silk and lace apparel to my thighs and then, since I involuntarily closed my legs, tugging it off me completely, frowning as she did so. She also attentively scrutinised my plucked abdomen, my sex, and the anal region, momentarily pushing my knees up against my bosom. The ointment had been entirely absorbed, the skin was absolutely clean, and Nawa-Na seemed content. However, when she placed her hand upon the vulva she had just examined in order to test its smoothness, my heart overflowed and again. I burst into sobs. Nawa-Na, for her part, began frowning once more, but without censure: it was, rather, as if she were asking herself the reason for all these tears. She said something to me and of course I did not understand.

'Don't touch me or look at me! The devil take you, you little black-skinned harlot!' I shouted at her.

As on the previous evening I instinctively tried to conceal my sex with one hand. At this the young girl seemed smitten with a brainwave. She laughed gaily, stood up, and keeping her eyes fixed upon mine, started unwinding the white material which served as her loincloth. I stopped weeping but my breathing quickened. The stuff fell at last to the ground and I could see Nawa-Na's own vulva. To my utter astonishment it was as smooth and naked as mine, and without the slightest trace of hair or down. I confess I looked upon it with enchantment.

It seemed shorter than my own but more pronounced, the configuration of its subtle internal lips better hidden by the outer ones, and of a dark brown colouring which, by the crease of the anus and at the edges of the rounded sexual cleft, verged upon a delicate bluish-black. I must here make another admission. It is that Nawa-Na herself, and especially the proud and luxuriant vaginal mound accentuated by the unfettered fragility of her little breasts, seemed to me at that moment unspeakably beautiful.

We remained thus for a few seconds, fascinated and truly enchanted: I unable to avert my gaze from Nawa-Na's sex, and she with an enigmatic smile and in a sort of drunken stupor staring back at me as I stared at her. When I could no longer bear it, I clasped the girl's thighs, holding her adorable haunches in my hands and caressing her rounded buttocks of warm brown marble, sliding my fingers between them until they all but touched the anus, and then, pulling her towards me, I thrust my mouth violently against her sex, myself now intoxicated with its plump rubbery consistency, and sinking within its molten depths. I grew to know its acrid scent of ebonywood floating upon seawater, and with my tongue I parted its secret lips and greedily sought that miniscule button which is sensitive enough to rise against a man's member and which nestles at the top of the cleft, as if peeping from under a hat. Nawa-Na smiled, her head cocked to one side.

'What is there to cry over?' she seemed to enquire. 'What do you think you are that I am not, that all other women are not?'

Oh Wicked Country

She did not in truth let me fondle her clitoris, but on the contrary closed her thighs, smiling the while, when her emotion increased. No longer did she wish to allow me to explore further, to lap at the very entrance of her vagina. On the other hand, she did not resist when I made her kneel upon the bed then lie full-length beside me and facing me. She continued to smile, shaking her head in amusement. My cheeks were aflame, my heartbeat seemed to increase in volume as if fanned by the blaze, and in a way I believe I was happy. I made her pretty breasts tremble and shake by stroking them first with the back of a hand then with my whole face. I nibbled and sucked their delicate brown tips, pointed as the noses of little rodents. This time too Nawa-Na drew back and pulled away from my lips at the moment when her breasts were growing hard. She took it upon herself then to mimic each of my movements. I again gathered one of her breasts, placing my mouth thereon, and striving to engulf it whole as though consuming a lemon or an egg. She permitted me to try – and this was wonderful, for her firm flesh filled my entire mouth – but again retreated, leaning over to take one of my own breasts in her mouth. It seemed to me as if the nipple would touch the back of her throat. Yet the moment a profound convulsion was about to seize and annihilate me, she expelled (as it were) my breast from its moist warm refuge.

I kissed her upon the lips and she smilingly returned the embrace. Here she was very unskilled, for the natives do not know our way of kissing. I turned around in the bed and did what she had previously forbidden, penetrating her vulva with my tongue. To start with she permitted me to do so, until I disclosed that delightful tiny button of hers, whereupon she repulsed me without force, but so as to adjust her own position (and she had the suppleness of a cat), kissing my own pubis, then darting her tongue inside my vulva too, up and down, back and forth. This time the crisis shook me and a first throb of pleasure flooded my sex. But Nawa-Na broke off before the spasm could repeat itself. As she was bringing her face close to mine I boldly thrust my hand between her thighs and plunged my middle finger to its full length inside her vagina. I could feel she was no longer a maiden, or perhaps had never even been virgin in the physical sense, and it also seemed to me that she was narrower than I and might spend less copiously at the crisis. Without forcing me to remove my finger, she herself slipped her hand between my thighs and penetrated me with her own, unleashing another ripple, a further small cataclysm which made her laugh.

'My dirty little black harlot', I told her. 'You, my beloved, are disgusting and shameless.'

I then withdrew my finger, and taking advantage of the fact that her own blissful juices had moistened it, placed my hand behind her and plunged the selfsame finger as it were to the hilt in her rear passage, whose tiny eyelet seemed immediately to close and contract around it as if to hold it therein. Its strength and silken resilience quite melted me. Nawa-Na imprisoning me inside her, lost no time in imitating me, and she too sank her finger within my corresponding part, as deep as she was able. Then paroxysms wrenched at my very depths, I flooded myself, grinding my teeth, and well-nigh lost consciousness.

When I awoke from this state of torpor as drowsy as a long gradual rocking in the sunshine, two calabashes of fresh water stood on the ground near the bed and Nawa-Na, standing over me and clad in her loincloth once more, was proceeding to wash and dry my face, hands and sex. She turned me over to wash me between my buttocks and, when she had finished, playfully gave me a light slap on the bottom.

After this, however, instead of dressing me as the other women used to do, she left me naked, and drawing me to my feet, simply took my hand and led me from the hut and across the *pah*. There were many natives there, men as well as women. As soon as I was outside the hut and found myself amongst them, shame at my nudity, especially at my vulva – swollen, provocative, still warm from pleasure and exposed as if I had shamelessly intended it – returned with dreadful intensity. My gorge rose as this shame numbed and blinded me, pressing inexorably upon my temples with the horrid stealth of nightmare. The natives ran up. The women would bend down and actually interrupt our progress, crouching or kneeling, the better to feast their eyes on my intimate areas thus revealed. The men, while keeping their distance rather more, were quite as inquisitive for all that, and inspected me with similar intensity.

The sun shone less fiercely upon the *pah* than it

had the previous evening. A fine intermittent drizzle blurred its rays, at the same time as it refreshed the undergrowth, and I believe it was in order to shelter me from this slight shower that they guided me beneath the gigantic branches of the *kauris* to the central clearing. At the very place where that convex bed had stood the preceding day and upon which I had been compelled to lie so they could depilate me, I now saw another. This time the bed was flat yet far higher than was normal, at least in those climes, being almost as high as the average grown man's loins. Moreover, one end of the bed, where the sleeper's feet would rest, was deeply V-shaped, as if to enable someone to stand within this notch and so overlook or watch over whoever lay there asleep.

Nawa-Na exhorted me to climb upon this strange construction. I obeyed and lay down upon my back, though slightly turning my body and keeping my legs to one side. I did not want to have to spread them apart by placing them on either side of the identation, nor to let my legs dangle stupidly over the edge, had I lain quite straight along the middle of the bed. I felt immodest enough as it was, and vulnerable enough also, with my sex thus displayed to the natives' gazes as though served upon a tray.

Nawa-Na, however, was very conscious of my modesty - or my distress! Taking hold of my shoulders without letting me up again, she gave me to understand that I should move down towards the end of the bed. Again I had to give way. I contented myself with closing my legs completely and disposing them very much to one side of the identation. But that would evidently not do, nor was it what Nawa-Na wanted. She started pushing and pulling me, still flat upon my back, until my haunches reached the very edge of the recess, with my legs almost touching the ground at the inmost part of this groove. Then she bent over, seized both my feet and hoisted them aloft, simultaneously parting them, which forced me to bend my knees again, this time in the air. At length she placed my legs fair and square on either side of the identation, planting them vertically at the sloping extremities of that sort of narrow crescent shape cut out of the bed. A long shudder ran through me, as if I were dying of cold even under that sun's heat, and it seemed my whole skin and private parts were afflicted by gooseflesh. In such a frightful position, thighs open, knees bent and raised high, not only was the aperture of my vagina offered to every eye and touch, but I also felt it was yawning apart, actually laying bare my innermost organs.

I did not have long to wait. The first native to approach didn't say a word but walked round the bed unwinding his loincloth. When he was naked, his prown pego erect and quivering, he advanced into the identation of the bed and in a moment I felt the hard marbles of his testicles twitch against the entrance to my vagina. Scrupulously, or perhaps from some notion of refinement, he withdrew just long enough to press his lips against this secret approach, which had no effect but to make me contract the more. No doubt he was mocking me. Standing back, he grasped his shaft and speared me with a single thrust.

He was quite potent, but of merely average length

and width, and he still violated and almost wounded me because everything in me revolted against his intrusion. Perhaps because he had not copulated for a long time, or the sight of my sex together with the kiss he had just bestowed upon it, had so greatly excited him, he scarcely moved in my vagina, but started forward and spent almost immediately. Had he reckoned upon my own ecstasy, he, like the first of his compatriots who had penetrated me, must have been thoroughly disappointed. The same mistake had been made the day Nawa-Na had spanked me over her knees. It was, of course, simply that having myself so delightfully and lately spent, while discovering and delving into a young girl's body as she was exploring mine, I could not help but be cold and insensible to any other advances.

The tribesmen, but also the women and children, were observers of the spectacle. To tell the truth, none of them seemed very impatient nor greatly roused. When the first native withdrew his member, which had turned limp and forlorn again, its glans, now crumpled, shining under its gloss of pleasure, they all watched him while he went over to a pitcher full of water and began washing himself, rather than look at me. The man's seed (what with my position of helplessness whereby I could neither close myself up nor hold it in) trickled out of me, oozed between my gaping buttocks and loathsomely anointed my anus which was quite as conspicuous as the vaginal orifice. The women, who had not the slightest thought of helping me out of this position, confined themselves to wiping me with their little sponges and handfuls of grasses, finishing by the application shortly afterwards of an unguent, probably a vegetable essence which was icy cold. I supposed it had some astringent property and that they were at some pains to have me contract as much as possible, by way of restoring, albeit approximately, a maidenhead for the benefit of the next buck.

I was an object and I was obliged to serve. The tribe, thanks to the fortunes of war, had inherited this plaything or, put more simply, this new receptacle. They had fed and watered me, adopted me and bent me to their will in every way, washing me, beating me, removing my hair. Now the time was ripe to use me. After all, do human beings in our society make use of one another any differently? To the *pah* and the tribe this novelty was amusing, even refreshing, but it was not, for all that, an affair of State. I was there at hand, available, boasting an unusual skin-colour and perhaps many other subtler differentiations, so they would place me with my vulva aloft and penetrate me without more ado. That would afford the husbands a rest from their wives (if savages marry, that is) and everyone, married men or bachelors, a change from their familiar fantasies.

I am certain that if I were a man I could not bear to enter a sex, to sink my own member into a vagina heated and flooded by another. But that apparently was of scant importance to the natives. Throughout the morning, a succession of customers presented themselves. There was only just time enough between bouts to sponge and rearrange me somewhat. I felt myself to be as soft, inert and uninviting as a damp cloth. A man would unwrap his loincloth, grasp (with that sort of affectionate clumsy pride men reserve for such moments) his compact and swollen organ, or his long thin one, his mushroom-like member or his still half-limp shaft, and be it inventive, curious, restless or strangely squat and weighty, would with a single thrust stab it between my thighs. These would part slightly, but my loins, well cushioned by leaves, remained relaxed because I would not exert myself nor do myself any harm, and so I felt almost nothing.

Certain men, as if it were their customary manner of making love, lifted my feet and compelled me to wedge my legs in their armpits before they penetrated me. I must confess that in this position, especially when the weapon was quite long and vigorous, penetration, though not affording me real pleasure, did move or at least affect me. I would feel the yard ascend and perhaps even reach the neck of the womb - a foreign body given the strange privilege of inhabiting another body. Happily for myself, if you will, the man would always withdraw and yield place to his neighbour before realising that he could have and might well have, overcome me. Then the cursory wash and the chilled compress returned me to my former state of indifference.

In spite of the generous shade of the trees, the rest of my body was very hot. While I was being penetrated I was conscious of being awash with perspiration, particularly upon my face and breasts, in my navel, and between my shoulderblades and loins where these pressed into the leaves. Little by little a variety of tiny midges or mayflies began to glue themselves to this moisture. At intervals Nawa-Na and a companion would approach to mop my brow or even wipe my torso and stomach with other sponges dipped in spring water. While so doing, Nawa-Na would turn her back upon the savage who was preoccupied by distending my vagina with his appendage and she would bend over me, smiling. At one such moment, she deliberately leaned over far enough to brush my naked nipples with her own. I had a horrid fear that this would excite me and precipitate my crisis, so I made as if to spit in her face, then closed my eyes and would no longer open them. However I had just the time to see Nawa-Na scowl furiously.

When they had had their fill of fucking me, they all went about their various occupations or left for other amusements. The women lifted me off and conducted me back to my hut, making slow progress because they understood (although I was reluctant to betray the fact) that the lower half of my body weighed heavily as lead. I felt nauseated: it was as if the sticky male fluids spent within me swilled sluggishly about my insides as in a marsh. Before even arriving at the hut, I broke free of the women trying to support me, and ran and hid behind the first available tree. There, squatting, I voided as powerfully and thoroughly as I could, so as to expel the greatest possible quantity of such abomination, and even the merest remembrance of it. Casually glancing over at me, one of the women nodded - it

seemed to me with something resembling appro-
bation. Then she addressed some words to her
nearest neighbour, who immediately retraced her
steps, perhaps returning to her own hut.

As for myself, they forthwith laved me with
especial care, from top to toe. They gave me to drink
as much as I wished, and indeed I could not even
slake my thirst. They also brought me - upon
wooden or bark dishes, and on receptacles that were
huge hollow shells and held the more delicate
cuisine - a more plentiful repast than hitherto. I
was not very hungry, only thirsty, and they
prevented my touching any food for the time being.
Until, that is, the young woman who had separated
from the group and to whom I earlier referred,
herself returned. She bore a curiously shaped vessel,
tall-sided with a sort of long spigot or pliable tube
tapering from its base and apparently made from a
liana or that supple wood we in England call
viburnum. In this tall container there simmered an
opalescent milky liquid rather like that inside a
fresh coconut. Looking at it revived my thirst. Yet I
was not to drink it, at least not in the proper sense.
The women, unusually, had left me standing while
they washed me, and they then bade me kneel beside
the bed, the top half of my body lying on it and my
cheek resting upon my folded arms. My knees were
slightly parted so that once more I found my
hindquarters jutting above my torso and spread
wide.

The young woman who had brought the bowl of
fresh water was called Ta-Lila and I often saw her in
Nawa-Na's company, which suggested that they

were friends. She was standing by, holding the pitcher, and I thought that at some point she would lift it again, hoisting it on to her shoulder or even atop her head, native-style.

I had imagined that the end of the spout of liana was simply tapered to a point. Actually, its tip turned out to be a kind of very extended, hollow and rather flexible nozzle with a clearly defined curvature. While I speculated about this instrument's purpose, one of the women knelt by me, spread my posteriors somewhat wider with her palms, and I had the sensation that my bowels might next open of their own accord. But another woman fed the tip of the endless syringe into my sphincter and began very slowly to insert it. Because of its curve, which must have closely corresponded to the body's internal anatomy, I felt it slide well and truly into my very innards. I had not understood until that precise moment · that the women intended giving me an enema, and when I felt that cold thin object, so extraordinarily long too, penetrate my backside then slither inexorably within me, I could not suppress a cry of dismay. Even in England I knew of clysters and enemas only by hearsay and had never stooped so low as to receive one.

Ta-Lila laughed gaily at my fright, while a companion gently patted my buttocks and vulva. Another then came forward and tilted the vessel, thus creating considerable pressure, so that its liquid gushed straight into me. I would be lying were I to maintain that this treatment – once my initial terror had faded – was disagreeable. I felt the strong jet swirl into my bowels, beating against their walls, and my stomach was gradually weighed down with all that coolness. From time to time the woman kneeling beside me, who had spread my haunches while the others introduced the crude syringe, would slip her hand just under my stomach so as to check its tension and weight. She would then address her companions, doubtless assuring them that they could continue. I enjoyed the contact of her palm, which seemed thus to be supporting my now grossly swollen belly, and I purposely leaned against her, trapping her hand between it and the leafy mattress so as to make her understand that I wished her to keep it there. She laughingly consented and once again gently patted the entrance to my vagina, just below the syringe nozzle.

It seemed that the women were injecting an astonishing quantity of the milky solution. My belly was balloon-shaped, and its entire weight was pressing against the mattress and the young native woman's hand, yet I felt disappointed, half-cheated, as it were, when they decided to desist, and not ungently retrieved the long syringe from my bowels and anus. I felt the urge to stand but was so swollen that I was afraid of not being able to contain myself if I moved and of somehow virtually exploding. But the young woman nearest me placed a hand upon my shoulder, leaned on me tenderly and stroked my bottom for a moment. I gathered that she meant me not to budge and to control myself a few moments longer. During this time Ta-Lila and her companion must have refilled the container with fresh water or some herbal infusion and affixed a shorter but considerably wider nozzle than the first to the tip of the tubing. They then introduced this within my vagina and again I could feel the liquid swirl and course through me under pressure. But it no longer weighed me down and I had no need to strive to retain it.

The sexual orifice, save when for one very specific reason it contracts, is organically far larger and looser than the rectum, but it need hardly be said that the vagina itself is less capacious than the bowels, so that most of the liquid simply cleansed it and even gushed out again past the broad syringe. At last the women removed this latter, also. They raised me cautiously to my feet and I only just had time – staggering as if intoxicated – to get through the hut's opening past which one of the women had ushered me. Behind it, amid the ferns, I hastily squatted, off balance, and almost reeling from the unaccustomed weight of my stomach, to expel from my vagina, but especially – and with ferocious force – from my anus, all the liquid with which I was bloated. Such details are indeed shameful, indecent, even, if you will, dirty. Yet I had the sensation then of wholesomeness, instant regeneration, and of growing cleaner by the second. I had voided and thrust forth from myself every pleasure not my own, all insult and injury alike.

I rejoined the women in the hut. They washed me perfunctorily and yet with their customary attentiveness, so as to efface the last vestiges of that morning, then they gave me clean drawers. They wished to clothe me fully, but it was I myself who spurned my other garments. I was very well as I was, and I felt young and fresh. It pleased me that my breasts which, it seemed, interested men so little although I myself considered them attractive, should be quite unfettered. I installed myself upon the bed, propped against a sort of bolster of foliage, and fell greedily upon my meal. The women had carried off everything used for the irrigations. Ta-Lila and another came back to keep me company. I remember wondering briefly how and why it was that they were never jealous. What the menfolk were giving me, after all, even though it was with a contempt verging upon indifference, they were nonetheless deprived of themselves. Then I dismissed the question.

Ta-Lila amused herself by offering me morsels, or replenishing the shell I was using as goblet, and once or twice I enjoyed doing the same for her. It was of course only a game. Out of courtesy I even went so far as to ask her the Maori names for different things. I would point out an object, call it by its English name, then raise my eyebrows while I looked at Ta-Lila. Then she in turn would give it a name. Finally I indicated one of my nipples, which was bouncing and dancing at my every movement. The young girl laughed, took it in her lips and suckled at it a moment, then placed one finger upon her own breast and uttered a word. That too I have forgotten. Yet, as Ta-Lila had done, I followed suit, sucking at the very tip of her breast as if it were a miniature comforter, and when it budded forth gradually and delicately, that made me blush. She had breasts of a size and rotundity unusual for so

young a woman, also with very rounded nipples
and of a delightful pinkish-brown colouring.

Ta-Lila and the other woman left me alone for
the siesta hour. In my drowsy state I dreamed of a
valley – of very soft contours and tints – whose
plenteous vegetation was blessed by the mildness of
its climate. However, it was bathed in a sunlight too
hot for it to have been my own country, and the
landscape seemed too wooded for England. Yet I
had recognised it … It had been a distant, pure,
nostalgic vision, inaccessible perhaps, and extraordinarily poignant. Even as I dreamed, I began to
weep, as if I had been at my mother's breast. Then I
dreamed about a horse. A wild white stallion,
rearing in the green grass of the valley, arched
against the sky. And he, the plumed king of the
sunshine, with his glorious mane and silken sheen,
was so fine that I smiled. Yes, good day to you,
mother England, never farewell – and greetings to
you too, horse of my ecstacy, splendour of my freed
bare breasts, steed of my pride!

The leafy panel was pulled aside and the bright
golden light speckled with blue-grey rain and
filtering the sea-green reflection of grass and trees,
shone through. I reopened my eyes and beheld
Nawa-Na. Without quite knowing why, I con-
gratulated myself on the fact that she had not been
present when I was given an enema. Perhaps it was
because of my incorrigible need for tenderness, my
desire to love and be loved; this exists, after all,
within every single uncorrupted human being, and
I had observed its operation in one of her

companions. My physical instincts, if not my tenderness (which is of course blind) warned me and reminded me that Nawa-Na with her cool, ready smile, had ultimately only driven me to humiliation and suffering.

Despite my dislike, which I nevertheless did not dare show too openly, the young girl immediately pulled down my drawers, again examined my pubic area and sex, positioning her long thumbs between my lips in order to hold them apart, then, after turning me upon my stomach, she also inspected my buttocks, spreading them similarly so as to see my anus. Satisfied, she clicked her tongue almost imperceptibly and drew up the smallcloth.

Nawa-Na led me thus attired from the hut. My breasts swung and bounced, and it was with distinct embarrassment that I sensed my buttocks too moving freely under the flimsy cotton. Suddenly I thought about my bare vulva, and this caused me to blush. In a curious way, the fact of having retained my drawers made me the more aware of my nudity.

We turned our backs on the assembly-place and the mountains. Nawa-Na was leading me towards a hut nestling right over on the other side, somewhat tucked away where the trees were sparser and bushes, ferns and the undergrowth as a whole were not so tall. There seemed to be few men in the village that day. The drizzle had stopped since my awakening, and the women and children were busy with their usual jobs and games.

At length we reached the hut, stituated on its own and slightly apart from the rest, and protected from either too much sun or rain by a tall clump of trees.

Oh Wicked Country

Patches of light dappled the thick stretch of grass and a layer of fallen leaves surrounding this dwelling-place. As I was enjoying the feel of the grass and of the warm humus beneath my bare feet, a very tall and powerfully built native emerged from the hut. I recognised Ra-Hau, the man I had always taken for the chief, or one of the chiefs, of the tribe. Despite his gigantic stature and muscles that looked exceptionally firm and almost sculpted, he in fact had a very well-proportioned physique, strapping and broad-shouldered, with pectorals like a bronze shield and shapely buttocks divided by the tightly-wound loincloth whose whiteness set off his brown skin. A fine animal, I thought, confusedly recalling the stallion in my dream.

Ra-Hau had long, nearly shoulder-length, black hair, a rather broad face with slightly flattened cheekbones. He was also somewhat flat-nosed, but his eyes were large and alert, ebony in hue, and his lips were finely chiselled and sensitive. He smiled with apparent good humour when he saw us, and then, without going to the trouble of asking us inside or even addressing Nawa-Na, he immediately began unwinding his loincloth. When the apparel fell, his sex stood quite erect, a creature both animal and noble like its master. I have always maintained, more so now than ever, that it is impotent men and frigid women who concern themselves unduly with the length and thickness of a member. True pleasure, like real happiness, is only an emotion after all. I could not, however, help but notice the generous proportions and fine appearance of Ra-Hau's endowment. It was like a stallion itself,

71

rearing to touch his navel, and twitching and bucking as if it had a life of its own and was an independent entity quite proud, self-contained, solitary.

Ra-Hau, after pulling down my drawers with a single casual gesture, did not bother to remove them completely but made me face Nawa-Na, bending over, with my hands grasping the young woman's hips to keep my balance. Supposing that he was going to run me through there and then with his terrible engine, I confess I could not help trembling. But the wrathful cobra-head of his member was content to rub softly between my thighs near the entrance to the vagina. Ra-Hau at once drew back and took the time to explore me by finger. I well knew I had contracted. Even with a single finger, no little effort was required to negotiate the outer ring and sink deeper. All things considered, the enemas which had so distended, and in a way refreshed me at the time, had left my entire stomach and loins in a state of vague, tingling irritation. It might be said that after these treatments and the morning's events, there remained just this smarting sensation of emptiness, or rather a lack of feeling, a profound disaffection, as if the physical side of the day were over or, to put it otherwise, as if my heart itself deemed that it were.

Ra-Hau withdrew his finger also and pulled me upright with one powerful hand. His air at once incensed and disconcerted, with eyebrows furrowed and close-knit, he examined his finger and then his sex; the latter, like Ra-Hau himself, disappointed, lowered its heavy head in a series of sly little jerks, the which prompted a loud and quite unexpected laugh from the athletic native. He appeared to muse awhile, if indeed these people do reflect in the same way as ourselves, and I seized the opportunity to stealthily readjust my drawers. Then he spoke curtly to Nawa-Na. She clapped her hands and at once went into the bush.

'Oh no!' I said, suddenly horror-stricken.

She returned shortly with one of her infernal switches, Lord knows what strong and supple wand she had managed to strip of bark. My posteriors tightened despite myself, and all the more so when Nawa-Na bestowed upon me one of her odious smiles, while her huge olive eyes sparkled with a sort of contentment or idle amusement. Despairingly I turned towards Ra-Hau and pleaded silently with him, but he affected not to understand. He shrugged and indicated that I should obey Nawa-Na. The young woman took my hand, while I barely suppressed my urge to hurl myself upon her and thrash her to within an inch of her life, and we went and sat down a few yards from the hut upon a grassy mound, where the first trees began. Like that in the middle of the *pah*'s assembly-area, this hillock could serve as bench. Then she arranged me across her knees, and in order not to change the routine deprived me of my only garment.

I waited, contracting my muscles with all my might, for the stick to strike, although I knew that the more I did contract the more frightful the pain would be. In spite of my shame, I tried turning my head towards Ra-Hau to implore him a final time. He had followed us and was contemplating my

73

naked buttocks with delighted fascination. The moment I knew – sensed – that Nawa-Na's uplifted arm was poised to strike, he raised his own hand imperiously to stop her.

I saw that he was debating anew, with some intensity, while his splendid sinewy virility upreared itself in all its glory. Just as he had done earlier, Ra-Hau bent over and with one hand raised me to my feet. The feminine undergarments still about my thighs seemed to vex him, and he tore them asunder, flinging them aside. Then, in a loud impatient voice he said something to Nawa-Na. I swear she blushed beneath that brown skin. Her dark eyes flashed, her jaw muscles worked and twitched and she shook her head violently. But Ra-Hau, drawing himself up to his full, enormous height, his shoulders and massive chest solid as the carved facade of some temple, insisted with even more authoritative vehemence. As for myself, it was especially while I was looking at his sex – quivering upwards by his belly and straining like a sail in the wind – that I sensed the huge savage's irresistible impatience and frantic haste. Nawa-Na, in her turn, had to yield.

She flung me a truly murderous look, made me sit upon the grassy tumulus precisely where she had previously installed herself, and, as I stared at her in surprise, she lay face down (that face still suffused with rage) across my thighs and knees. I have already stated that the natives have a sort of devilish intuition into what others are thinking. Ra-Hau, who clearly wished to ready me and doubtless (to be frank about it) to find me melting within when he penetrated me, had guessed that this state of readiness would be attained the more quickly and surely by allowing me, for once, my turn to thrash and humiliate Nawa-Na, rather than vice versa. And it was only too true, my heart immediately beat the faster for joy, and already a preliminary *frisson* seemed to stir at the lining of my womb.

I had some difficulty removing Nawa-Na's loincloth while she lay across me. Yet I felt amply rewarded by discovering in my turn, wide open upon my knees and thus displayed and denuded, her warm little flanks: the delicate puckering of the anus, a pretty hue of golden-brown, and the blurred, slate-coloured crease of her sex. Nawa-Na, knowing she had surrendered, still strove just as I myself had done to protect herself, but I only required to raise my right knee a jot in order to expose her anew. She had a truly delightful backside, her *derriere* at once narrower and more protuberant than mine, less fleshy and voluptuous. Her skin too had a tauter, more highly polished texture, yet it was (and this almost made me jealous) more velvety, softer.

Ra-Hau proffered the thin branch which would serve as rod but I did not wish to employ it. I do not think I have ever been of cruel disposition. In any case, that method seemed far less sensual or satisfying than simply to spank Nawa-Na as one disciplines schoolchildren in England, the way she herself had beaten me that first day. I therefore eschewed the rod and, drunk with joy, began to apply to those insolent cruppers the most forceful rain of blows I could muster. I wanted Nawa-Na to remember this thrashing to her dying day.

I beat her without relenting, my palm slapping crisply and fairly rebounding off her adorable hurdies for what seemed an interminable time but was in truth but seconds, since I was well nigh swooning with pleasure while administering the beating. Under my blows her rounded buttocks sometimes furrowed like a face and sometimes seemed to give way, turn limp, yawn wide open – as supple and loosely relaxed as the hide of a glove. At such moments I also took advantage of her humiliating defeat, keeping my palm absolutely flat and hitting the softened membranes of the anal and vaginal areas, even going so far as to stay my hand just before striking her, the better to savour the scent of fear which she exuded.

I must admit that Nawa-Na put up a longer, fiercer and more determined resistance than I myself had done when she had disciplined me. Indeed she maintained an obstinate silence for a very long time, while the purplish-brown blood rushed to the surface of her skin, that velvet taut skin of her hindquarters – as when wine seeps through a pastel-tinted silk. And she continued silent, no doubt grinding her teeth, stubborn as a goat, merely tensing and relaxing (following an increasingly rapid rhythm, in a vain attempt to escape the blows or to weaken their impact) the charming hemispheres of her buttocks, themselves alternately swollen, protruding or slapped flat. Ra-Hau, bending over us, was by now so tremendously turgid that I thought his enormous prick might burst apart.

He shouted an order at me, a demented entreaty, and I guessed that he was so moved by this exhibition that he dreaded discharging his delight into the air before he had even sheathed his weapon within Nawa-Na or myself. Accordingly I redoubled my fusillade and laid into her with a will, whereupon (at last) giving a violent heave of fury and despair, the young woman burst into tears. When once she had started she could no longer restrain herself: tears turned into cries, then to groans and sobs. But she herself had thrashed me thoroughly enough for me to know that she was just then beginning to wet herself and spend copiously. I was very tempted to interrupt the chastisement and plunge my hand into her vagina so as to experience its orgasm. I would have wished in some sense to steal it from her.

Ra-Hau left me no time for that. His sculptured torso was gasping like a bellows and he all but pawed the earth in his impatience. He hoisted the pair of us up with a single movement. Nawa-Na was still trembling all over and shaken by spasms both from her beating and her crisis, her features distorted and tear-stained. He thrust me opposite her with my hands around her hips and my mouth pressed against her bare vulva, so that I too found my buttocks spread and sex proffered. At the very instant, moreover, when I felt the heady and acrid fluid from Nawa-Na trickle between my lips, Ra-Hau's mammoth totem pole delved between my nether cheeks and stabbed me to the very vitals. It seemed as if he were through me quite and was actually beating at my heart. Ra-Hau who was indeed a stallion, emitted a vibrantly loud 'O, O, O!' just like the neigh of a horse, and I myself, almost simultaneously, ravaged by a transport of pleasure which seemed to turn my vagina inside out, uttered a long wail which the small, chubby and soaking vulva of Nawa-Na, though it covered my mouth, could not wholly stifle. With savage jolts my loins responded to Ra-Hau's violent thrusts until the point of no return when everything burst asunder in us both. The earth – within my womb – exploded against the sun, while the pulsing volley of Ra-Hau's seed shot through me, riddling then filling me with his ecstasy so that I too violently discharged along with him.

The three of us, Ra-Hau, the girl and I, rolled over upon the ground in a tangled, exhausted heap. As she collapsed, Nawa-Na put her arms around my neck. Less devastated, and since she had spent earlier than we, not so profoundly engulfed as Ra-Hau and myself, she clasped me desperately, her mouth on mine, my fair hair and her black hair entangled together.

My life in the *pah*, and among the natives too I may say, changed considerably after I thrashed Nawa-Na and was fucked by Ra-Hau. When, for instance, I returned to my hut, I refused to don one of my underthings to replace the garment Ra-Hau had torn. Nawa-Na had gone somewhere in the village to conceal her shame, perhaps to one of those large huts in which the men, given one side, and the women, allotted the other, would at times get together. I gave the women from these huts to understand, when they washed me, that I no longer wished to wear my own underclothes and wanted a loincloth like theirs. At first they laughed uproariously, for the idea seemed to them quite absurd. Then they grew vexed. In fact one of them, as if she considered Nawa-Na should be avenged, even went so far as to put me across her knees and well and truly fustigate me in time-honoured fashion, while my thighs and loins still trembled with the pleasure Ra-Hau had given me.

I was relieved, while I endured this further misfortune, that at least Nawa-Na was not present and could derive no consolation therefrom. Afterwards however, I had the idea – assuredly a happier one – of invoking the name of Ra-Hau himself. The women began laughing heartily again; my tormentress executed my punishment to the bitter end, and once more my bottom was raw and sensitive … Yet they did not fail to set about acceding to my demand. When I was on my feet and they had washed me anew, they carefully wound the piece of material about my loins, and I was at liberty to retain it as long as I pleased.

Thus attired, I found myself somehow more freely accepted by the village, even in its daily routine. At dawn and at different times during the day women would invariably enter my hut to wake and wash me, to bring me sustenance, and to adjust

my loincloth or remove it in readiness for sleep.
Quite often they would persist in using force. They
would decide that I needed thrashing or washing,
and I was obliged to submit. But on the other hand
it was sometimes enough that I refused their
services: they occasionally let me alone.

When Nawa-Na again began visiting my hut
with her companions, she no longer dared resist or
even make as if to resist any of my injunctions. I
myself beat her as often as it took my fancy. When I
would begin unwinding her loincloth she would
blush beneath her chestnut skin and despairingly
avert her gaze from the other young women; yet for
all that, she would never struggle. I planted her in
leisurely fashion across my thighs and beat her till
she burst into tears. Often, when I lifted her up
again, she would take my hand and kiss it, then
embrace me fiercely, her face buried between my
breasts.

Once, with Ta-Lila and another, we gave her a
thoroughgoing irrigation, first placing her head
down upon the bedstead with her adorable little
arse in the air. I must say I took a keen pleasure
when myself inserting the long syringe into the anal
sphincter and plunging it, in my turn, deep within
her bowels. Nawa-Na began weeping, panic-
stricken, when I had scarcely introduced half of it. I
nonetheless continued with the remainder and we
so filled her so that her adolescent belly inflated like
a balloon. One might have mistaken this for the last
stages of pregnancy. She wept the whole time.
When at last we led her outside and permitted her to
deflate herself, I played at keeping my finger inside

her vagina while she rectally expelled all that milky water. I found it an entrancing tableau. I even bent across to suckle her tiny breasts at the same time. Afterwards, as was her wont, she came and nestled into my own bosom, her slender back shuddering with childish sobs.

Yet it was when I was strolling through the village that I especially realised that my position, my status therein, had changed. In a word I was no longer really or completely a stranger. If I were to sit, or rather crouch, beside women pounding grain, grating tubers or retting flax or some such plant, I would not go so far as to affirm that they would invariably greet me with wholehearted smiles. Yet even among themselves they do not smile freely without specific occasion. And they would quite unaffectedly pass me a pestle, a carding-comb or a grater so that I could share their tasks.

I greatly enjoyed accompanying them to the spring, situated in a sort of rocky hollow or miniature amphitheatre at the outskirts of the hills. The luxuriant tree-slopes surrounded this little waterfall. I very soon fell into the habit of bearing the various kinds of jars and pitchers upon my head, as the native women themselves do, although to tell the truth for the most part I had to resort to balancing the vessels on one shoulder. It amused and pleased me to note that this method of carrying burdens is largely responsible for the Maoris' superb breasts, as well as contributing to the grace and nobility of their general deportment. I daily saw my breasts – and not my bosom alone, but also all those ligaments between neck and shoulders, which evidently support and shape the former - grow firmer and assume a pleasing muscularity and proud motion. I should add, for I conceal nothing, that without losing their femininity my buttocks too became at once sturdier and more compact, by reason of my walks through the *pah*, the bush and neighbouring hills, and because of the exercise I was taking.

The spring was, to a certain extent, the women's special preserve. There they would play and gossip endlessly among themselves. They used to strip naked, as women do when they want to feel free and relaxed, in order to frolic in the crystalline fresh water, and also to make comparisons with one another and discuss their preferences concerning such or such a man, or what in themselves their menfolk especially cherished. On these occasions I would do as they did, and go naked also. I would stare at myself in the water as in a looking-glass, and I grew to consider myself attractive.

When I experienced that variety of inner vacancy, that vague sensation of emptiness, together with the slight irritation both chill and feverish which characterises the need for sexual satiety, I would unashamedly head for Ra-Hau's hut. I have explained that it was somewhat isolated, and it seemed the other women (and men and children too) would not venture too close without express invitation, as if the area and indeed the tall savage himself were surrounded if not prohibited by a form of taboo. I had no need to reckon with that. Or at least, no one led me to believe I should do so.

Oh Wicked Country.

Whether or not there were natives in the vicinity – near enough, that is, to see me – before I even reached the hut, and without bothering about my arrival there or disguising it or myself in any way, I would start unwinding my loincloth. Ra-Hau himself was rarely at home. If I did not immediately perceive him, he would appear between the trees a moment later. Recognising me, he too would strip naked. His haste a little frustrated me for I should have liked to disrobe him with my own hands. This action, however, may well have been the subject of some sterner taboo.

By contrast, Ra-Hau was neither offended nor one whit astonished that I should immediately and avidly seize hold of his princely sceptre or his heavy, swollen dependences. Like most natives, he had a relatively hairless body, and it seemed as if I were imprisoning in my fingers a living stave of ebony or the strong, massy flesh of a horse.

One day when Ra-Hau seemed less inclined to pleasure and his sex lazier, I had the immoderate desire to take the latter in my mouth and suck upon it so as to excite the tall Maori. As for myself, I knew that to suck him thus would precipitate my own crisis. But Ra-Hau was too immense. I do not mean too thick; simply that his shaft was altogether too long. The tip alone distended my lips and could hardly enter between tongue and palate, so that it was almost impossible to exercise any suction without practically choking myself. To my great regret – since I found its taste and texture quite delightful, and its urgent, heavy tension as of an animal about to leap, made me giddy – I was obliged to remove it. I restricted myself to kissing it with ardent insistence, working slyly yet firmly upon the tiny slit at the tip of the glans, through which of course spurts the male liquor.

I achieved a result far sooner than anticipated. Scarcely a few seconds after I had started, Ra-Hau groaned like a wild beast; I felt throbbing in my palm and along his entire shaft the groundswell of his loins, and almost simultaneously he bucked, growled and the bronze cannon bespattered my face, then, as I instinctively recoiled, volleyed over my neck and breasts. Ra-Hau exploded with his giant's laughter - at that moment a curious hoarse vibrato. And although those warm and powerful jets had somehow repelled me, I experienced a feeling akin to pride. Similarly too, Ra-Hau belonged to me more intimately, more exclusively if I may so phrase it, by spending thus than by discharging his seed within me.

Generally speaking I was too impatient to give myself over to such frolics or refinements. I would seek out the giant because I needed stuffing, fucking that is. To see him naked and to recall simultaneously that I, an Englishwoman, subject like so many others to our own Queen, was staring at and lewdly contemplating this huge black nudity, sufficed to stir my need and lubricate the very place inside which would needs be satisfied.

Accordingly I would waste no time. I would briefly ensure that the amazing yard of Ra-Hau was in fine fettle and, as it were, working order, and then turn my back and bend over, thighs parted, supporting myself against anything suitable and available - tree, hut wall, or waist-high tree-stump. Then I would feel that unforgettable, always familiar, yet always new, sensation. The pintle which forcefully parted the tender walls of my vagina, poked me through and through, strong yet ever wonderfully gentle. Then all the supple circumference and length of that formidable shaft seemed truly to stop up the entire canal, the full orifice - and that unbearably anticipated, unspeakably desirable guest would have closed the door of a house built to order, for it was now inhabited to the very brim. Each time the furious task of trenching and the savage onslaught mounted by Ra-Hau would voluptuously lighten my loins before burdening my heart. I would match him blow for blow. Then, like waves flung up by a ship's prow, my body and soul alike were split asunder by my lover's prick. I unfurled on either side of it and finally as always the prow speared the sun and I would frantically spend my own pleasure, meeting Ra-Hau at the very moment he himself discharged.

I did it once too often, however. One day, instead of merely bending over, standing still, as I was in the habit of doing hitherto, I had the idea of bending completely double. I imagined that thus the mighty member of Ra-Hau might penetrate me more fully than ever, and that I for my part could grip him ever tighter, have him as it were at my mercy and engulf him, so that he would squander his adorable substance. After exciting Ra-Hau fearfully, and when his glans itself resembled the hood of an enormous pinkish-brown mushroom, I went over to the grassy mound on which I had

belaboured Nawa-Na. I climbed thereupon and
knelt over it, my back to Ra-Hau. When I knelt
down I had sat upon my heels, and I now prostrated
myself so that my face and shoulders touched the
very grass of the mound itself.

In this position, something like that I adopted
when the women were giving me an enema, but
with loins reined in rather more (which does not
feel disagreeable when one's body is naturally
supple), my head was much lower than my
hindquarters and these were thus wide open and
proffered to the weapon of Ra-Hau, standing
behind me. Bent double and tensed, I was well
aware he would need to rape me in order to effect his
entrance, and I prepared myself with the utmost
trepidation and anticipation, too, to withstand this
initial shock. But the Maori had a stern surprise in
store for me. For a start, instead of poking me
forthwith, he dallied, the head of his prick caressing
my vaginal orifice for a long time, up and down, to
and fro, exciting me so much that I was almost
beside myself.

'What are you waiting for, you great black
ruffian?' I gasped out in English, haltingly, well-
nigh drooling at every emunctory. 'Stop this
tomfoolery, brutish prick, and make haste to
transfix me! Get between my thighs at once, bury
yourself to the hilt, stab me, stuff me to bursting
point till *you* burst, hurry up and spend and make
me spend, you enormous fucking-machine, you're
not here to play around!'

And the barbarian, at the very moment I was truly
about to spend – through sheer phrenzy at not

managing to spend, decided to sodomise me. His monstrous shaft dilated my arse with awful force, stretching it until I feared it might split, and continued to push and thrust so that I could not suppress a piercing shriek and actually pissed myself from pain. He pitilessly ground at me until the rim of the enormous fleshy cowl had perforated like an arrowhead the wretched sphincter now atrociously distended. And suddenly just like the cork being expelled from a champagne bottle, the whole massy tip shot into my bowels and seemed to slide on towards infinity, propelled by the whole length and frightening weight of the prick.

The clyster, and the thin and elongated syringe which had so startled me when Nawa-Na inserted them inside me and which had made her weep so bitterly when it had pleased me to give her the same treatment, was a mere trifle compared to this violation. Words can hardly be adequate to convey it, and I now realise I have expressed myself carelessly. The fact is, you do not know what it is to be violated, plumbed and rifled in your very depths unless a male member – especially of Ra-Hau's size – has dived monstrously into your arsehole, opening it by force and lodging therein, entire, deep in the narrowest, most secret and private part of your body.

To tell the truth, the sensation is far more frightful when the shaft does not fill these depths as it can the vagina. After the initial rending penetration one might imagine the member had free play, to delve and frisk in a sort of limbo, yet at its entrance the arse remains stretched to the full, clamped round the root which it accomodates despite itself as if to grip it and prevent its departure, although this is the selfsame object torturing it and which it wished to reject and expel. You feel in your inmost recesses, then, this impression of emptiness, the maddening absence of contact of mucous membrane with mucous membrane, of flesh upon flesh (despite the fact that you do have it), and although you suffer intolerably it is perhaps through this very suffering that you become aware once again of the atrocious dilation of the arse. You would give your life to pluck forth this appalling intruder and at the same time you strive with your whole body to retain it, to feel it properly, since there exists nothing else you actually can feel – even if it involves being split and in pain.

Thus, instead of my remaining simply skewered and trying as best I could to lessen the pain by not moving and by yielding to Ra-Hau's enormous tool, while preventing him from moving inside me, I could not help shunting my whole body back and forth and consequently the anus, surrounding it, really resembled a ring sliding along an enormous rod. The instant I underwent the keenest pain I also experienced the most overwhelming pleasure. It happened when I had moved forward as far as I could, thus causing my lover's glans to withdraw as far as he was able, to the anal periphery, so that while he was churning and beating at the interior, distending it a little more, he was about to burst out again with a final wrench.

Oh Wicked Country

At that precise second when Ra-Hau's shaft was at its hardest and thickest and was, so to speak, backing out of my backside's tightest grip, about to re-emerge and slip from me, out of my body and soul and into the unrestricted air, the pain became terrible and I uttered a ghastly cry. Yet this same inner shock, on the inside of the doors that close my own body, shook me from head to toe, submerging me in a single frenzied convulsion of bliss, and at the very centre of all the pleasure and pain I regained the strength to buck back towards Ra-Hau and around his tool, which was his body and soul also, to grip it, prevent its escape, swallow and engulf it with my anus anew, and again to feel it slide slowly all its length along and into my deepest being.

Ra-Hau himself no longer contained his whinny-ing groans of mingled pain and delight. I had succeeded in sucking back his member progres-sively, and even more effectively than I could have done with my vaginal muscles, and he must have had the momentary sensation that I wanted to devour his entire organ, snatch it from his loins and cram it irreversibly inside myself. When I forced from him, or extracted, the quintessence of his bliss, like the juice of some fruit crushed between the fingers, he uttered a veritable scream and I too shrieked. I felt with shattering clarity the scalding jets spurt forth, as if luminously spattering the dark caverns of my body. As on the first occasion when he fucked me, I rolled over upon the grass immediately the shaft, like a rubber band stretched to breaking point and then snapped back, shot from my fundament. Ra-Hau foundered, sinking back as though pole-axed.

After the treatment this monster had meted out to me, the women were obliged to tend me for several days, employing poultices of healing and astringent herbs. Even walking was difficult for me, while the thought of being buggered again made me shudder. Not only was being thrashed, or letting a man come near me, out of the question for the present, but the womenfolk, fearing I might tear myself, would not even allow me to satisfy certain needs in the normal way. They relieved me by means of irrigations – these compounded of vegetable juices and oils. Then, when the mucous membranes regained their firmness, I was massaged regularly during the day.

To tell the truth, I loved this. The lavages douched and completely cleansed my insides. When I was thoroughly clean, they bore me out of the hut into the sun and stretched me out face down upon one of those large low beds so dear to the natives, which was well upholstered with foliage and aromatic plants. One of the young women, using her fingers and palms expertly, relaxed my own shoulders and arms. Another, seated sideways upon the bed, massaged my back and loins. A third palped my calves and the soles of my feet – this last sensation being especially exquisite. The most skilled woman concentrated upon the entire region injured by Ra-Hau, working round it and approaching gradually, using thumbs alone, and little by little arriving at the anus and vagina. I must confess

that I happened to spend a few times – this occurred
when the magic fingers moved from the circum-
ferences of the sensitive spots to directly upon them.
The native women exclaimed gaily, assuming that
this was clear evidence of the treatment's efficacy!
My bottom was patted by way of congratulation,
and the youngest girl, tender and playful, dipped
her fine features between my thighs and lapped, like
a little cat with her tongue at the vulva's secret folds,
the shimmering liquid of my delight.

Later, when I was quite recovered, and had once
again become an object – a luxury if you will – at
the natives' disposal, I realised that provided I were
sufficiently stimulated, I would myself grow moist
within the rectal region, almost as copiously and
spontaneously as I did within the vagina. Even the
enormous Ra-Hau himself, when he took me again,
never had to resort to butter, coconut oil or similar
substances, in order to lubricate and prepare me. On
the rare occasions when I was too dry and tight and
he would have wounded me still more than I might
have incommoded him – a spanking generally
sufficed. He would see that this was administered by
the first woman to hand, or else I would strip and
spank one or another of them myself. On the one
hand there are few sights more beautiful than a
naked female behind, and on the other, it is a fact
that violent emotions and even sensations readily
dispose one for love. I also perceived that Nawa-Na
and certain of the married women (although it was
rarely the case with very young women) shared with
me this odd facility of anal access and lubrication.
As for the rest – and not only the youngest but also

many married women – they had to be violated each time, cruelly and with difficulty.

It was now taken for granted that I belonged to the *pah* and to the village, and also that I could entertain myself by thinking it was the village which belonged to me. Clad only in my loincloth or occasionally, through whim, fully dressed in the English style, I would wander at will, joining in the various occupations, distractions, and chants – those of the men and the women strangely different, but the inevitable accompaniment to most work, especially the most difficult. As the Africans in particular seem always to have appreciated, rhythm relieves toil. We English, and most civilised Whites, believe that dreams inhibit action and at the same time evade it.

The one thing I had not the right to refuse – and this was at the very heart of the system, or if you prefer, the convention, of this reciprocal arrangement between the village and myself – was a man's desire. By receiving me into its bosom the *pah* had in a way acquired an extra woman. The *pah* fed me, housed me, washed me and allowed me to live. It followed quite logically that I was the property, or again, if I may put it another way, the plaything of all the *pah*'s members. I was jointly owned, held in common. Wherever I found myself or might walk, no matter how I was dressed or whatever I was doing, the first native who appeared had the right to press his claim, and it was equally well understood that I could have very few reasonable excuses for repulsing his advances or evading my obligations.

Oh Wicked Country

The Maori in the aforementioned mood would drag me into his hut, lay me down upon his palliasse, rip off my loincloth, or hoist up my skirt and petticoats and drag down my drawers if I were in lady's attire, and would fuck me to the finish. Indeed, he was allowed to do whatever he wished. He might poke his prick into my mouth or my arsehole, sometimes even between my breasts, obliging me to press the latter myself with both hands at once, thus trapping his own instrument, and by means of simple movements back and forth, to make him spend in this manner. Or he might quite simply lie atop me, or imprison my thighs in his own armpits and thus pillage my vagina. The next time it might be dog-fashion or again the so-called missionary position. I suppose however that this refers to Papists, for our own clergy are generally broadminded, or else pederasts.

When the native was particularly lustful or impatient, on, on the contrary, if his desire were somewhat lethargic and required further excitation in order to rouse itself from torpor, we would not go as far as the huts. Whatever the numbers, ages or ranks of those present, I would be undressed and used shamelessly. Divested of my last stitch of apparel, I would be leaned against a tree in Ra-Hau's favoured style, or made to crouch upon all fours, or with my back wedged against some grassy mound and my legs spread wide apart and pointing at the heavens. I was either fucked or buggered in these postures.

When one of the Maoris was in particularly good humour (or feeling especially generous, perhaps), he would shout out peremptorily and several of these unbridled swine would appear. They had discovered, apparently with no great difficulty, a fine new team game which afforded them the chance to pit three against one. All four of us, they and I, naked as the day we were born, would use for the purpose that natural bench upon which, quite soon after my arrival, Nawa-Na had given me a thrashing.

The best-endowed native would sit down on it and install me atop him, astride and face to face. It goes without saying that by means of such proximity he sank deep into my vagina. My torso pressed against his, I would rest my head on his shoulder, my cheek touching his, and a second native, kneeling behind him, would take the opportunity of sliding a big brown cock between my lips. I would begin to wonder how I was to breathe, and used to grow so anxious that my breasts would squeeze against the chest of the seated fellow upon whom I too was seated, or rather impaled. Yet at that very moment the third acolyte, who had remained standing behind me, his feet planted in the grass at the base of the bench, would plaster himself against my back, taking advantage then of the enforced spread of my buttocks in order to sheathe his own dagger to the hilt in my arsehole.

I confess that this last penetration was acutely painful, for the obvious reason that the man who found himself in the vagina and attacking frontally, would in effect tug its muscles towards himself, distending it and drawing it in his own direction and simultaneously creating a pull and a tension at the anus. And the pedicator, meanwhile, was having something of a similar effect, pulling the sphincter back towards himself and distending it too, but in exactly the opposite direction. It might seem that not only the orifices, but the perineal area itself, so sensitive and delicate, would split and tear under the tension. However, if the three men synchronised and adjusted their rhythms and the progress of their pleasure, so as to spend approximately all together – one ejaculating copious jets of jissom into my mouth, while he I straddled discharged his within my vagina and the third, glued behind me, spent into my very bowels – then I too would reach my crisis, coming with such a raging and luxurious spasm and such a ferment of my own juices that I would remain utterly exhausted for many hours thereafter.

But I continued calm and collected. There is, indeed, great tranquillity in the certitude of belonging to all. This is not merely the reverse, reciprocal certitude – all belonging to each. It is because this twofold assurance (in reality, only one, and warm as cock in cunt) does away with egoistical thoughts. I believe, moreover, that egoism is the most disturbing, irremediable source of fatigue. In other words, it is solitude. The *pah* surrounded me as the vagina does the cock, and the muff warms the hand in mid winter.

Oh Wicked Country

One evening and night at the *pah* there was a sort of festival, perhaps marking a change of season or the beginning or end of a tribal activity – fishing, hunting, sowing, hut-building or God knows what – and numerous men claimed their rights over me. But the day had been too long. I only wanted to sleep, to age a little and make time pass, to have time to myself and regain my own life.

It goes without saying that I had to yield to the first natives who chose to drag me out of my hut or fuck me there and then without obliging me to move. Yet, as I have remarked, they seldom copulate thus. For the most part they crouch with the woman's legs in the man's oxters, thus deeper penetration can be achieved. Anyhow, the first customers were disappointed: I could be no more than a passive, dehumanised receptacle for men's spunk. One need hardly add, also, that they tried to rouse me from such passivity by all the usual oafish means. They dressed me, in order to have the pleasure of removing my drawers publicly, with myself bent across the wooden frame in the middle of the village. They beat me again. This would superficially inflame my fugo, without jolting my indifference. They were even cruel enough to have me flogged by Nawa-Na, and I shrieked with pain at that. Yet if that succeeded in arousing one or two males who found me smoother, more supple, or my parts more heated immediately afterwards, I just as soon relapsed into a well-nigh invincible apathy. So they summoned Ra-Hau and consulted aged crones. One of these witches, after various confabulations, scuttled back to her hut and brought in either hand, as if they were particularly fragile treasures, two whitish waxen balls which rather resembled, as to shape and size, eggs. In my exhaustion, I scoffed at the natives' foolishness.

'I dare say they want to graft testicles on me now,' I reflected. I found the thought absurdly exciting and could barely contain my nervous laughter.

They soon disabused me of this notion. The horrid old hag, after entrusting her treasure to one of the women muttering in the firelight, once again stripped me to the altogether. After that she sat upon one of the natural benches and laid me across her knees. Happily, old women thereabouts wear more modest apparel than the younger ones. I did not in the least wish to touch her wrinkled skin. When I was stretched out with my hurdies exposed, the crone stroked me with some skill, massaging with palm and fingertips first the convexity of my haunches, then the cleft between them and the rectal region and finally, intercrurally, the vaginal crease itself. All this with such light, cunning delicacy, the pressure only increasing imperceptibly, that despite myself I relaxed and lay open. Then, using one of the savages' favourite tactics – just when through fatigue, forgetfulness or sheer corporeal relaxation, I felt my chink yawning wide – the abominable old witch smartly retrieved one of those eggs of firm, buttery consistency from her neighbour and thrust it vigorously into my rectal canal.

I confess I yelped with fear, shock and anguish. It distended my orifice appallingly at first, then, once inside me its ovoid form and the sphincter's reflex action seemed to propel it along the narrow

intestinal passage with frightful celerity. I felt it was
going to lodge like a projectile deep within my
belly. When the pain diminished slightly, again
carelessly, I let all my muscles relax. The old
harridan immediately took the opportunity to
plunge the second egg between my thighs. Like the
first, it shot inside me and seemed this time to travel
as far as my womb itself. This time the old woman
gave me no time to scream but pulled me to my feet
with a shake.

Maddened, and conscious only of those twin
abominations clogging my guts, I lost all modesty
and made violent efforts to expel them, flexing my
knees, pushing till my thighs quivered and my
stomach seemed to knot. In vain. The two eggs
seemed glued to my very innards, at the walls of
womb and intestine. I howled with fright yet again,
and the women clapped their hands while the eyes
of the men lit up. Then as I strove to push and
contract with all my strength, it seemed those ovoid
bodies inside me lost their hardness, consistency
and even their shape: it was as though they were
melting, penetrating yet lapping at my most
intimate flesh. And for as long as they melted and I
unwillingly absorbed them through all my mucous
surfaces (if that be the term), a sort of murky fluid,
a liquid fire started impregnating me wholly,
running sluggishly throughout my veins, mingling
with my blood. Even my efforts at rejecting and
expelling the hideous objects only hastened this
diffusion or invasion. I continued shrieking cease-
lessly and the clapping grew to a phrenzy. The fiery
fluid, after stinging like a giant whiplash laid

across my entire frame, started to settle and became concentrated with desperate tenacity upon my nether parts fore and aft.

I have a childhood memory of embarrassment and distaste the first time I overheard a servant use the cryptic yet clear epithet 'fire down below'. I was now in the same straits. I could have sworn my entire privates were afire and blazing bright scarlet. The pain however had become bearable, although it felt as if a damped-down brazier was smouldering inside me. It made me grit my teeth and I wanted to run - seeking water, grass, air, the night - whatever might simply alleviate that monstrous furnace, if that were possible. The women clung laughing to my arms to hold me back. I felt myself going mad. Yet the ancient witch had not acted without forethought. When I realised I could not escape, my body of its own accord seemed to understand how it could obtain relief.

Using all my strength I broke free of the women's hands confining me and leaped at the first native within reach. Fortunately he was naked and the mere contact of his nakedness gave me fleeting solace and a promise of more. But the wretched lout, whether from shock or because my demented onslaught had moved him to helpless laughter, drooped as I touched him. At which, freeing myself angrily once more from the women, I frigged him frenziedly and as soon as he was fit, forced him inside myself. I think he must have thought he was being assailed and violated by a burning bush, for his eyes started from their sockets.

I literally danced upon his root, indifferent as to

whether or not he worked away. At the same time I was baring my teeth like a hyena at Ra-Hau, too busy and crazed even to utter his name. He understood and proceeded to plaster himself against my back, fiercely parting my buttocks and buggering me in the same motion. I thought my hinterland would explode, yet I was never so content nor so satisfied as when his enormous engine speared my guts. It was in truth like drinking when thirsty. Rapidly, all too rapidly, spitted upon their two prongs, I squeezed from both a double flood of fluid, simultaneously draining their reservoirs. The two bucks' jaws dropped and they rolled their eyes like sots.

The flame still burned me, however, and had rekindled of its own accord under the soothing but transient exudations. I unceremoniously sent the two rods packing and rushed anew at the first native to catch my eye. This time the others prevented my raping him. They seized and flung me upon my back on the fatal bench, bending my knees back to my bosom. I gasped and panted still, not from pleasure, but goaded by the infernal burning sensation. The men commenced fucking me almost one behind the other. There was no question of washing me that night. I even wonder whether all my blades took, or had, the time to spend. One might plug my main avenue as best he could, and despite my position I would all but unman him, draining his loins as if intending to rupture the fellow. My teeth went on chattering, I was almost foaming at the mouth when a quite new cock, whose mere heat seemed thirst-quenching, truffled its blind way to the core of my inflamed membranes. Then, from impatience and dementia, the instant this meagre relief began to dwindle, I nipped the male bud with a spasmodic constriction of my nether lips so as to suck forth all his essence and reject him. Another replaced him at once, or rather was now ensconced between my bum, grinding my hinders. By means of a vigorous twist of my hips and an abrupt and forceful anal contraction I managed to drain him as promptly as his companion. The women were even obliged to sit upon my arms and hands to prevent my joggling the bollocks of these halfwits like a bellringer while they were fucking me.

That night, of my own free will (if that is the right phrase) I believe I disposed of more than half the available men in the tribe. 'All the perfumes of Arabia will not sweeten this little hand,' my father used sometimes to quote. The vaunted virility of any troup of men imaginable would not wear out the little vulva of a woman.

I was dead beat however. I seemed to have been flailed with iron bars. At that moment they might have torn me to pieces or had me covered by an actual stallion without my making any attempt to defend myself. Above my head the stars in the sky were false currency, tinsel, ground glass – and even the huge protective shadows of the mountains behind the hills and trees presented only the purely conventional backcloth of a diorama. I did not weep: my eyes were as dry as my soul. All that was left me of sap, flesh, living substance, was that awful masculine fluid between my thighs.

At last the women deigned to wash me and when they did so they spared neither water, vegetable unguents nor variegated scented herbs. When I was clean, one of the old women - perhaps the same one, perhaps another, it scarcely matters - examined my private parts, particularly their membranes. She muttered while carrying out this examination, so some traces of inflammation must have persisted. At any rate I was constantly aware of this – a sensation deadened yet not quite extinct, like dilute quicksilver coursing through the filigree of my veins. I had suffered so sorely earlier, and I found I was so fatigued that I no longer even gave way to despair. I felt nothing but a tiny gnawing, a dull irritation of sorts, no longer concentrated upon my private parts but more generally seated in my mind and body. The old woman, nevertheless, seemed ill at ease or discontent. She mouthed some command addressed at Ra-Hau. I was still lying upon my back.

Ra-Hau at once approached, turned me upon my stomach, parted my thighs and lay full length between them. I hoped, with renewed dread, and with despair too, that he would not press his advantage home yet again, knowing full well that now he would no longer bring me relief. But that was neither what he himself had in mind nor what the old woman had directed. Ra-Hau, with his colossal strength, lifted my legs, which he placed on either side of his neck; put an arm around my waist, and stood up, carrying me in this way, with my breasts against his belly and my head downwards. My cheek rested flush against the enormous bulge of his plenipotentiary and its seals, although I was scarcely concerned with this triumvirate and still less so at that particular moment.

He however, his own face between my straddling thighs, and my love lane below his lips, suddenly began lapping and mumbling me with long, slow and deep licks of his tongue. I thought yet again, then, that nothing and no one had ever been so gentle with me. From time to time he saw to it that his tongue also foraged at the tender and burnt-out crater of my fugo. But the best moment of all remained that instant of sheer gentleness when it scoured my motte and slowly sank inside the font, exploring its recesses with that inexorable, exquisite insistence. Ra-Hau absorbed the smarting pain inside me just as Papist priests exorcise demons. And I also bethought me of one of those monumental, patient, sympathetic cows back home in England washing a calf or chewing the cud. Ra-Hau likewise employed his long tongue and did not withdraw it nor set me back upon my feet until he had cleaned away all my soreness of body and distress of mind. I began weeping. Men, women and even a few children were dancing around the fires.

Two or three young women took my hand and led me back to my hut. My tears turned to irrepressible sobs immediately I crossed the threshold and the young women wished to leave me. Ta-Lila was nearest me. Her eyes, I know not why, also looked moist. I flung my arms about her neck and pressed against her.

'Don't leave me, don't leave me,' I sobbed out.

As if by a miracle, it then seemed to me, she

returned my embrace. Her companions departed. Ta-Lila began unwinding her loincloth and as soon as she was as naked as myself, we lay down on the bed. Before falling asleep I cried for a long time in her arms, my face between her breasts.

I often wondered when I first arrived at the *pah* how it was that the women were not jealous. However animalistic they might be, I told myself, they must surely see that I am taking from their menfolk (or that they are giving me) pleasure, time, sperm, emotions if you prefer, which are not reserved for themselves. An occasional thrashing or a forcibly administered enema, and the generally wretched spectacle of my humiliation: did these seem to them sufficient compensation?

Yet I did not know the natives, the women in particular; the men at least penetrated me otherwise than with clysters. I knew nothing of their feelings with regard to time or pleasure: or, if you prefer, their view of human dignity.

The way in which they behaved with their companions, and in which, to be precise, they used them, might well have enlightened me. I have related how they treated me, in public and in private, and that in England one would not even dare behave thus with a child, or perhaps not even with an animal. Humiliation, then, wounded me far worse and cut deeper than my outraged body and invaded privacy. By the end I should have realised that it was not merely with myself alone that the natives in general and the women in particular, took such wild liberties.

For example, I once saw a very young woman, to whom her husband or lover was (at a cursory guess) refusing his services or too loftily making her request them, peremptorily deprive the offender of his loincloth, place him astride her lap, and give him the same sound thrashing she had on another occasion meted out to me. The man in question, lover or husband, was six or seven years older than herself and by no means a weakling. He boasted the same proud demeanour and broad chest (developed by toxophily and the hurling of spears) common to the majority of his kin. However, he had no thought of defending himself, nor did he even protest. All he did was glance through the doorway of their hut, looking furtively around with some embarrassment while the incensed young virago stripped and set about him. Indeed they were very soon reconciled.

When she gave him leave to stand, he was in fact standing already, stiff as a ramrod, and I just had time to see the young woman hastening to unwind her own loincloth and take advantage of her slothful consort's improved disposition. To effect such a disposition had perhaps been one of the reasons for, or even the purpose of, the fustigation. It might also have transpired that the young wife or lover was in a temper and, once angered, had determined to take it out there and then upon the backside of her lord and master and that the aforesaid lord and master had to submit to her humiliating and stinging satisfaction. I am very sure that it only improved their fuck. I am also quite certain that such a prelude could not but have helped remove from his own performance the idiotic pride, or rather, foolish pretention which every English husband or lover never fails to display soon after the act. Finally, it could equally well be that the athletic savage might beat his spouse if necessary. But she would have been no more disgraced by that than he had been, or would himself be; nor would he have been prompted to brag about his natural gifts, whether it was a question of musculature or of appendage!

It now seems obvious to me that this scene alone, glimpsed by chance as I wandered on one of my strolls through the *pah*, should have sufficed to enlighten me. Yet I was still too conscious of all our own classifications and hierarchies. These, especially, serve to trump up so many of our emotions and feelings. It was several days after the charming scene I witnessed that I discovered the women's hut. It resembled another large hut whither the men would repair when they wanted to be on their own. The difference, or so it seemed to me, was that among the men only the bachelors were wont to use this communal hut. Whereas the women's hut contained, as well as married women and those who had lovers, widows, (merry or otherwise), spinsters, and virgins. I do not know if there was much talk of women in the men's hut. Yet, doubtless there was. After all, one cannot always talk of hunting and fishing. By contrast, there was scarcely ever a mention of men in the women's hut. It was as if the world of women were self-contained and could contain (and thereby ignore) that of men. The male world, however, needed constant explanation and justification (through fishing, hunting, conquests martial and sexual) of its own existence in relation to the world at large. Thus men make war, fish, hunt and strive to make or unmake love, while women simply live in the world and enjoy its uses without philosophising.

If one or another in the great communal hut were to weary of this excess of femininity, it seemed futile and especially pointless to discuss it. Quite simply she would go out and find herself a husband or lover, the first male in sight, even if it happened to be another's lover or husband. It was also quite permissible in such huts to lie close to one's friend and keep him or her warm, or equally, to frig them without preamble if perchance they should require it. Among themselves the women did not bother about men – although they far outnumbered them, or perhaps it was precisely because of that. 'He fucked you yesterday, I shall beat him today and he will fuck me tomorrow.' The only ones who are jealous, after all, are those who feel themselves inferior and resent it. Much later, when willy-nilly I had learned some words of the Maori tongue, I tried to explain to one of the native women what (for us at any rate) is meant by rivalry, jealousy, competition. She shrugged her bare shoulders indifferently:

'But why? Men are our brothers,' she said.

'And are you their sisters?' I asked her, irritated by her response.

The assumption made her laugh, and her eyes betrayed a sort of amused scorn:

'Of course not, we are sisters only among ourselves!'

I laughed also. There is always some obscurity – for a civilised person – in the clear words of barbarians. Now however, I seem to understand exactly what the young woman was saying. Despite all our differences, she and I were of the same blood – of the same earth, if you will. Men are only a race of men.

So after that night when I begged Ta-Lila not to leave me on my own and slept in her arms, I too would visit the women's hut more and more often. Even during the day it was very rarely deserted. Immediately I entered I would strip naked. The other women were also nude like myself. We lived, slept, played and we made love together: it was wonderful. Nor did this love claim to rival or compete with the other participants or with what one experienced with a man. We did not even dream of that: it was quite a different love. Or, if you will, it is another method, another realisation of love, since love is not of one kind alone. For ultimately all bodies are but parents, sisters, brothers ...

Nawa-Na was nearly always to be found in the women's hut whenever I entered it. I never quite knew if a passing fancy had originally led to a habitual voluptuousness in Nawa-Na, so that she became imperceptibly cruel, or whether on the contrary, it was a particular innate tendency towards cruelty which had always made her abandon herself to every sensual experience. Nawa-Na's bright, slightly chilly and enigmatic smile and her dazzling dark eyes fascinated and drew me like a magnet. Quite often, even before my arrival she had succeeded in annoying or tiring the other young women there, and they had decided to punish her, almost as if to provide themselves with entertainment.

A huge low bed or gigantic divan occupied one entire end of the hut, from wall to wall. This was our playground and siesta place, reserved for relaxation and caresses. On one corner of this bed Nawa-Na had been spreadeagled, her wrists and ankles tied with sashes so she could not bring them together, and an enormous banana wedged into her exchequer. Too long to penetrate completely, a good third of the absurd fruit projected from her thighs, accentuating the outer lips of her nether mouth. Nawa-Na did not even attempt to expel this exaggeratedly penile object, but remained obedient, or at any rate motionless. From time to time her womb contracted, heaving beneath the satin skin of her abdomen, and her eyes would sparkle like carbuncles. She still retained her faint savage maiden's smile, however, at once disdainful and tender.

I hated her and yet she was dear to me – or perhaps I just desired her. I ran to her, and freed her delightful dainty and adorably distended stomach, which was stretched like a tiny golden drum, from the frightful fruit. I untied her bonds. Nawa-Na did not display relief nor make any acknowledgement. As soon as she was free, she turned me on to my stomach, spread my legs, sat upon my thighs, and did not waste a moment before scratching, pinching, spanking me and pedicating me in my turn with one of those silly bananas.

Or another time, if she thought of it, she might lie down behind me, ensuring I was lying flat on my stomach (for apparently she liked to see me in this position) and would press her face between my thighs and suck at my *mons* and its mouth until I almost lost consciousness. She would literally devour my own pleasure. Fortunately the other young women – while respecting Nawa-Na's whim, for the natives, as I've said, scarcely issue commands other than in jest – were quick to deliver me from her, much as I had previously rescued her from their own playfully vengeful clutches.

The atmosphere of the hut was above all simultaneously intimate, warm and friendly, as it must of course be among those who neither oppress each other nor are crushed by a world, society or system outside their own. One might put it this way: inside the hut – whatever they might desire or seek when they found themselves outside – the young women were sufficient unto themselves, and they enjoyed such sufficiency.

We served each other as lovers while, if I may express it so, remaining available to the whole group. For this community itself gave each one of us her autonomy and individuality. The lover is not only the one to open our thighs but also the one who fills a space in our world. We only perceived this very gently, with a complete absence of fear and bitterness, inside the hut. Women truly are gentle with other women, as long as no man intervenes – man who is obsessed and haunted by claiming the lion's share, perhaps because he so fears being merely the lamb.

We would make love without haste, for it is also true that love destroys time. Our bodies intertwined, hearts beating close, moved to a common pulse. Without haste or strain we would embrace in groups and time was nothing but the warm, slowed beat of our hearts. I discovered then the sweet and delightful bliss of feeling a woman's nakedness against my own.

As I have noted, the natives do not exchange kisses, properly speaking. However, the entire body is brought into play, it caresses and is caressed by the whole of the other body. It is only too obvious that the flesh has a spirit. Simply by demonstrating a little patience – something Nawa-Na was reproached for never showing or understanding – I would gradually discern in our embraces the breath of the lover lying in my arms, and the shape, texture and taste of her lips. One woman's breath, no matter how pure, is quite unlike another's. I would assess the softness or firmness of her breasts against mine, their roundness or conical shape, their nipples, mine, hers, her breasts sometimes deliciously spread as if to be penetrated and her nipples sometimes rising and stiffening like tiny rodents, pointing and rubbing their muzzles against one another. I would appreciate the exquisite weight, the light hollow or the delicate swell of a female belly against my own.

Women indeed lie voluptuously, one upon the other. Unhurriedly each would thrust forward the pelvis and loins so that our mottes met. It is clear that I now no longer hate the love of men. But I maintain that real kissing is just this: one woman's unimaginably sensitive vulva touching another, the folds of her lips gradually opening, uncovered, as they press and part and seek each other's inner petals, pistils and heart. Yes, one simply needs patience. One nude pubis meets another as if cheek to cheek, and when cunts kiss there is a sort of penetration, not obvious, yet somehow very distinct and deep, without deception or cruelty, and which reaches one's very soul. And I also came to appreciate the roundness of women's thighs, the hard, polished almonds of women's knees, the subtlety of women's ankles and the strange but comradely contact of women's feet which flutter in their excitement like tiny birds.

And while I would be clasping my lover in my arms and she holding me, another woman lover would lie against my back, holding me in her arms too. I smelled her whole body, with a different sensation. Her warm breath upon my nape and by my ear. Sometimes she would bite my ear, simply keeping it a long while between her lips. Her breasts were wonderfully crushed against my shoulder-blades, where a man never thinks of caressing a woman, as if there were nothing there for himself. The truly exquisite swell of her belly would fill the small of my back. The *mons* and vulva nudging at my nether cheeks, trying like a butting billygoat to part them.

There was one game I adored. I would relax and decontract as much as possible so that my bottom lost its firm convexity and spread somewhat, opening loosely. Thus as she curled into my back, my friend's vulva exactly met my anus. Her core of nakedness against the core of my nakedness. I used to shudder with keen delight. Then, considering I had been caressed amply, I would close up tight once again, the buttocks' tender insistence very softly imprisoning and nipping the lips of my lover's vulva. She, however, did not try to escape but would press her sex still harder, deeper into me. I would spread and tighten my nates, alternating the tension. Then her breathing would quicken and grow fevered. I too would pinch the full lips of her organ faster and faster and with increasing insistence. My lover would gasp, I would draw from her a tiny cry, a little melodious groan, and finally a limber convulsion when she reached the very acme of her bliss and spent in those warm rear straits of mine, so that I felt (or imagined I felt) mingling with my moistened tingling membranes, the suave wetness, the delicate musky sap of her own secret parts. And then too, her paroxysm would speed my own apogee, I would moan and the lover I was holding in my arms would in her turn place her vulva over mine and seek that very pleasure I could give her, since I had just induced it, and she would receive it in exchange.

It sometimes chanced that we might dally more brutally. We might have exhausted the initial tenderness we felt, during the time allotted, and we would seek another sort. In this way one always wants to go further, deeper into the being one loves, and this incessant excess, itself always exceeded, properly constitutes love. We lay on top of each other, facing different ways. So I might sup, as

interminably and greedily as I could ever have
dreamed, at the spread thighs of my lover, her sex
like a draught of inexpressible oblivion, while
between my thighs she sucked at mine. With my
tongue I would scoop and probe her cloven inlet
and she would explore my own. I drank her flesh,
her fluid, her female quintessence and she, mine.
Our savours, scents and tastes entranced and
intoxicated us. I believe woman is the very spring of
the world: from her flows life and sleep, all memory
and forgetfulness.

When we had temporarily drained this spring, we
would fight. Women too need to make war, as they
make love, to give a little peace to men, who are so
jealous and proud of retaining the rights upon bad
will. Laughing like children we would victimise
each other as a means of exorcism. We would league
together against one individual and all but
suffocate her while stuffing between her legs and
arse long pink bananas or another fruit, a sort of
black leathery curved pod which resembled the
European carob. Whether from pettishness or
defiance Nawa-Na would refuse to participate in
these games. She would purposely select the most
formidable pod and with her bum or cunt spread
wide, grinning irritatingly, would transfix herself.
She would go on manustuprating conscientiously,
making love to herself (if I can call it that) with the
aid of the fruit, feigning to spend while rolling her
eyes, and curling her lips back to expose her teeth.

Sooner or later one of the young women would
decide to seize her and give her a beating. She might
weep momentarily, her little buttocks raw, before

ejaculating still more gently, her muscles becoming soft and supple and, displaying a shyness no less false than her rages, she would solicit from one of us the right to kiss a throat or sex. I always used to wish she would choose me: I loved her, after all. Sometimes I singled her out by force and she would laugh freely at this. Sometimes too a whole squadron of women would wage war by falling upon the others, pinching, biting, scratching, not to mention caressing and lying with anyone at hand. We laughed uncontrollably at our wild and tangled hair, our breathlessness, and at a scratch upon a burnished velvet backside or upon the intimate moist mushroom flesh of a pubis.

What I found most charming was the sight of two lovers carefully and concernedly – both smiling feelingly into each other's eyes – applying themselves to the task of mutual and simultaneous penetration with the same fruit. It might truly be said of them that they were making love. One of the loving couple, lying on her side, would take one of those extraordinarily lengthy curved fruits and insert about half of it between her own thighs, inside her commodity. Often her smile might waver for an instant, and droplets of perspiration bead her lips and temples. Then she received her reward. The other lover, also lying on her side facing her friend would contrive to slide the remaining half of the fruit into her own quim without displacing the section already in the body of the first. Thus the two friends found themselves linked together, communicating so intimately they were happy for long weightless, endless minutes.

Each movement, however infinitesimal, by either of the young women was immediately perceived by the other within her belly and even her womb. So they would dally tirelessly in order to spend by means of these movements, enjoying their slightest nuances, barely advancing and retreating, skilfully deploying their hips, pretending to want to reject the fruit uniting them or on the contrary, to try to swallow it wholly.

At other times they would play this game back to back. One would thrust half the fruit forcibly up her fundament while her friend, tentatively and adorably groping, would suddenly succeed in sinking the other half up hers. When they lay face to face, they would weep with emotion, stirred by such intense pleasure. When back to back, they did not weep, perhaps because they could no longer see each other and tenderness of heart and mind resides in the eye, yet their ecstasy, insidiously mingled with pain, sometimes tore a cry from them. And yes, we other women, hearing and observing them, were sometimes jealous.

The sun was extinguished by the bluish ashen rain of the islands. It was evening. Outside, everywhere around the hut, scents and even colours were heightened, somehow preceding the heavy cortege of vegetation and the caravan of hills on their journey into the night. Inside the hut there was a rank female odour. Our pleasure, warmth, happiness. I was less and less often inclined to return alone to my hut. I would stay in the big hut with those young women who did not care for a man that night. We were entwined to see the night through. Bats skimmed to and fro across the doorway, giving the impression of a piece of velvet momentarily twitched aside. The undergrowth breathed with an immense calm strength and a bird called before tucking its head under its wing. The leafy mattress, in its turn, emitted a keener fragrance now that darkness had fallen, as if it had a life of its own. All was well with us. The huge foliage of the night was lukewarm.

For me at any rate, Frank's reappearance was like a flash of lightning. I recall that that day I was unwell. Why not mention it, because I have after all filled this account with unmentionable details? I felt somewhat queasy, both heavy and lightheaded, my body fractious, my view of life discontented and darkened, disposed towards cruelty – although as I have stated, at any other time of the month I hate to cause pain, even more than I hate enduring it.

The previous night, because of my stupid condition, I had slept alone in my hut. I likewise washed myself alone, refusing the women's ministrations, and attired myself after the English fashion, with exaggerated care, even donning my stockings and shoes once more, although my feet had almost forgotten what these felt like.

The sun was dazzling, which worsened my ill-humour. When I resolved to go out, I soon saw that most of the men had left the village.

'So much the better!' I thought, my mood low yet bitter.

The society of women appealed to me no more than that of the menfolk, and the continual, eternal astonishment of the children when faced with my finery, did not even make me smile. I walked a little, feeling only contempt for all the games and diverse occupations. Anyhow, few games were being played. I seemed to feel a sort of impatience or nervous restlessness, not merely inside myself but diffused throughout the village. I despised it like everything else. I did not thank the young women who shortly afterwards brought me food, and I only toyed with the meal. I drank quantities of cold water which allowed me to sulk more than ever when all this liquid forced me to venture outside again. I was, finally, suffering from a minor female ailment, and this can be thoroughly vexing: I fleetingly bethought me of asking Ta-Lila or Nawa-Na to give me an enema to be rid of it. But I absolutely hated to be touched or even seen in the state and mood to which I found myself subject.

I sank down for a siesta of sorts that was a torpid sluggish collapse. Distant yet very distinct rifle shots roused me from it: I also heard the cries of women and children, excitedly rising and falling. The sun slanting through the foliage seemed of a blinding intensity and I could not countenance the idea of again abandoning the shelter of the hut, even for a few seconds. I went back to sleep – or tried to do so. The rifle-shots should have alerted me, however. In those days the natives did not possess rifles or carbines. Perhaps an hour passed, then the noise began again, a tremendous din, with yells and stamping feet, chants, calls and laughter. The men were returning to the *pah*. I rose and this time looked out to ascertain the cause of all this hullabaloo at the very threshold of my hut. Then I saw Frank.

Strangely, I was amazed, in my fever, to recognise him at once. He was being transported – as I had discovered from picture books – in the way that Negroes carry big game they have killed, or sometimes even their prisoners. His hands and feet were trussed to a long pole which Ra-Hau, and another native six or seven paces behind him, bore upon their shoulders. Frank still wore his white cavalry tunic, but had lost pith helmet and boots, while red blotches of blood and black powder burns soiled the front of his uniform.

'He is dead,' I immediately thought.

I experienced no particular emotion. This dead soldier came from too far away, or else I did, one might have said. When two dreams meet and unexpectedly clash, each destroys the other. I then reflected that if Frank was indeed dead, they would not have taken such pains to bind and transport him. The Maoris, who are not overly fond of work, dislike dead bodies even more than death it-self – which is after all only an accident or a form of life. Their dead tended to disappear suddenly, swallowed up somewhere in the shadowy suburbs of the *pah*. I assume that the old women and gravediggers of one sort or another take care of this side of things.

On that particular day, while the children

laughed, skipped about or clapped their hands, firing innumerable questions at and around poor Frank, I noticed their elders, especially the men, directing their glances curiously in my direction. They might possibly have recognised their prisoner as my husband, but I do not think so. For as we regard Negroes, so to them all Europeans tend to look alike. Or perhaps they simply saw him as a European pure and simple, and this fact alone was enough to arouse their curiosity since to them I myself was first and foremost a European, a White, and the coincidence must have seemed novel and rare. They must have avidly awaited my reaction. I therefore was at pains to display a studied indifference, and retired inside the hut as if to resume my siesta.

Towards evening however, I realised I should have to go out. I could not not be there if, for example, they decided to roast Frank. I was overcome with wild laughter. Not that I had any particular cause for merriment. The blame doubtless lay upon my stupefied and feverish condition. I concentrated even more painstakingly on my *toilette*, brushing my hair endlessly with one of the clumsy native combs, composing and examining my features and gazing at my reflection in the calabash full of water which I employed as a looking-glass.

'Yes, it is I, certainly it is,' I murmured, albeit in disbelief.

When I crossed the *pah* the sun was sinking behind the tall blue mountains, accentuating for a moment the hills burdened with trees before plunging them into night. Humdrum daily life, at once lively and slothful, seemed to have run its course. I inferred or rather guessed that the warriors would be feted and that the women would reclaim possession of them and they of their women. Fires were being lit. Only the children running hither and thither and shouting betrayed the unresolved tension, the restless fever of expectancy in the village. Moreover when children flung themselves at my skirts or their elders gave me a brief smile, it was with an almost absent-minded air, a distracted benevolence, quite unlike that of any other day. I only had to follow the children to run Frank to earth. They had untied him from the long pole and had now secured him, this time standing, with his back to the trunk of a young tree, near a hut I had invariably seen occupied. Naturally a number of men and women had followd me while I was following the children, in order to be present at this meeting. Frank stared, wide-eyed with surprise. His thick glossy brown locks on which he prided himself were all unkempt, which vexed me.

'You see that I am no phantom,' I said to him.

It was still light enough for me to see him blench.

'Stella! I thought you dead.'

'And I you. One always believes it is others who die,' I replied.

He looked at me for a long while as if I were mad. Then he glanced – in my view wildly, yet slyly too – at the natives deliberately dawdling and hanging back, keeping their distance from us. He lowered his voice like a child hiding from the schoolmaster:

'Stella, have ... do they respect you?'

'Much,' I told him.

Just then I felt I might be overcome with lunatic laughter, and I furiously bit the insides of my cheeks.

'Frank, are you wounded?' I then asked him.

He hung his head. His matted hair reminded me of a magpie's nest.

'No, no, just a scratch,' he declared.

I affected to be wary of the natives' presences also, looking over my shoulder once or twice, and Frank whispered very quickly, as if playing the conspirator:

'Stella! Tonight!'

I do not know why but, the moment he said this, it occurred to me that he, Frank, would be bursting into my hut during the night to fuck me vigorously and ponderously as in England. For a moment my whole body stiffened and I felt icy-cold. Then I recollected all that had happened since those days; I became aware that my body was naked under my garments, and, so as not to leave Frank quite alone, replied in the same tone:

'Yes, tonight!'

With which I turned my back on him. When certain he could no longer see my face, I fixed my gaze upon the naked breasts of one of the young women and smiled at her, showing my teeth as if I wished to bite her. She understood, smiled in turn, and also leaving Frank, accompanied me towards the centre of the *pah*. We spent a while, she, I and half a dozen others already there, inside the women's hut. Actually I needed to see if the young women behaved any differently towards me, rather more than I did their company. There was no difference. They were content to leave me for once fully clothed: the only reason for this was that they were women themselves and hence not unaware of my indisposition. We dined together, the natives as usual preferring to wait upon me than allow me to assist them or serve them. I led the girl at whom I had earlier smiled back to my hut. She stripped naked and I retained my undergarments and a short petticoat. I slept for some of the night with my face between her breasts.

Perhaps it was a kind of remorse which awoke me. I rose, dressed without waking my companion, and again crossed the *pah* to find out what had become of Frank. They had unbound him from the tree and I understood that he was in that hitherto inhabited hut. Several natives, men, were more or less on guard, some of them seated and conversing in low voices nearby. It seemed there were more of them within the hut, guarding or keeping watch over Frank. So I returned to my hut and lay down beside the still sleeping girl. She was warm and soft, relaxed and sound asleep.

The next day my body felt more alert, my wits keener. However, that feeling of unreality I experience with my courses had increased. Frank's reappearance or rather resurrection; the few words we exchanged; his position as the Maoris' prisoner - which I no longer considered myself to be: all strangely and acutely intensified this feeling. Despite myself I had come to believe that everything which had happened constituted only a sort of spectacle or show, put on for the sole purpose of distracting or diverting me or even moving me to sadness.

Obsessed with this, I washed and attired myself as if for a festival. I was ready to play a part in these lunatic festivities, even if my role seemed to me to be simply that of a spectator. After all, this is how one lives in most cases. I forced myself to have lunch, as though it had been some test. I told myself that I had not felt so strong since my arrival at the village. I thought about Frank, although this train of thought tired me. Then I crossed the *pah* again. Frank had been tied once more with his back to the tree. His beard had grown during the night, which vexed me almost as much as his overlong hair. The sun was already hot, the sky was as clear of clouds as my mind. I saw only a few natives in the vicinity of the hut and the tree: they were yawning and stretching like animals, or loosening up their shoulders.

'How are you?' Frank enquired.

'How are *you*?' I echoed.

I racked my brains wildly to think of another question:

'Have you had some luncheon?' I asked him.

His fine features, pale and dirty and darkened by stubble, tautened in a wry grimace:

'Yes, they fed me. They gave me something to drink. They drove me outside into the bush, like a dog. They washed me!'

He was bare-chested and I noticed that he had been freshly combed. On the other hand, they had given him back his cavalry breeches and even his boots, which someone must have recovered from somewhere. The natives are occasionally very disconcerting. As I looked at Frank's face and torso, trying to reaccustom myself, to readjust my sensibility as it were to that pale skin, a new and quite wretched expression twisted his lips, while his eyes reflected a kind of entreaty, a frightful confusion:

'Stella, what are they going to do to me?'

He flushed violently and turned away his head.

'I wonder,' I said.

His bulging eyes met mine again and as on the previous evening he stared at me as if I were mad. I felt ill at ease. Among the natives I hardly had to speak, after all. Frank, naturally, used the English language, my native tongue, which I had learned in childhood and spoken nearly all my life, and he was waiting, again quite naturally, for me to speak it myself. I was at last rescued from this embarrassing situation, but by that huge booby Ra-Hau, who in one sense added to its embarrassment.

As though his breakfast had put him into a capital mood, he thrust through the handful of natives beginning to crowd round myself and Frank (although they had so far kept their distance), and, head and shoulders above everyone, cast a completely indifferent eye upon Frank. He came to me, bared his flashing teeth in a smile and ended by taking me by the shoulder with his customary nonchalance and leaning me against a tree immediately beside the one to which Frank had been tied. My heart turned over.

'No, you fool!' I said to Ra-Hau.

Oh Wicked Country

Or perhaps I only thought I did. I stood up, for once, and turned round to face him. From the younger women I had learned the rather *taboo* word to be uttered primarily in a man's presence and signifying indisposition. However, in my panic it slipped my memory the very second I wanted to risk using it. I remained open-mouthed, blushing furiously. Out of the corner of my eye I saw Frank straining at his bonds. As for Ra-Hau, he only burst into his simpleton's laughter. He unwound his loincloth with one hand while with the other's steely grip he steered me back to face the tree and again leaned me over. I was obliged to cling to the trunk in order not to fall flat on my face and sully my gown upon the earth and leaves. Whereupon Ra-Hau saw to it that he lifted this same gown above my waist, pulled down my drawers, and while I was weeping with discomfort and the shame I felt – rather than from sorrow or anger – applied himself to my flanks and with a single thrust sank his mighty prick into my arsehole.

Someone, myself or Frank, cried out. The fear with which his presence and proximity so filled me, not to mention the lingering traces of disgust left by an indisposition, had as it were closed me unduly, so that Ra-Hau hurt me terribly. Yet the moment his monstrous prong pierced me I forgot that he had hurt me and even experienced a certain sweetness and warmth therein, together with that intoxicated sense of plenitude: I could relax again, allow him to advance and retreat, to fill me full of his swollen flesh and his seed.

I did not, properly speaking, spend. But as on

126

other occasions I had the sensation of being deprived, mutilated and deserted when his manhood suddenly weakened within my bowels and the enormous member itself softened, died, and with a movement as inexorable as penetration, retracted and left me once and for all. Incapable at that moment of standing upright, I waited, nervously holding on to the tree, for the women to wash and dry me and rub down Ra-Hau. My knees trembled. The women must have adjusted my clothing while big Ra-Hau, quite tamed, was rewinding his loincloth.

Then I saw once more – recognised – the contorted features of Frank, his eyes blazing. Fascinated, I took one or two steps towards him. His bonds cut deep into his wrists. Several times he tried to address me, or perhaps to spit into my face. There was a sort of whitish, dried foam encrusted at the corners of his lips.

'Whore! Filthy whore!' he finally exploded.

In a way his very rage fascinated me. But everything became easier when he had said that. Quite resolved to see me simply from outside, just from the exterior, Frank was perforce condemning me to my own role as nothing but a spectator. Perhaps, moreover, things had become easier for Frank too. Hate, like love, always seems to exempt one from judging. And what is truly intolerable is an ill-defined emotion or relationship between two human beings. It means that neither has managed to make a precise judgement upon the other. Frank now believed he knew where he stood. So, at the same time, did I too, by a pure and simple transference of his own assessment. He was judged by others in the same moment and according to the same process by which he judged me.

They untied Frank and taught him in picture-language – very graphic representations at that, with himself in the foreground – the side of my life of which he had hitherto been ignorant. That particular day they contented themselves with bending him over on the vaulting-frame, re-erected in his honour and well-padded with fresh foliage. They removed his breeches and several lads amused themselves by backscuttling him, for which they were hooted at by the women.

A little later, without even taking him off the frame, they thrashed him pretty vigorously with a willow-switch, no doubt to make him livelier or to punish him for having shown his displeasure somewhat too ostentatiously. I must confess I fled at that point. I have never liked being flogged, and as I think I stated, if anything I detest another being flogged even more. This despite the fact that the uglier masculine buttocks – those of Europeans, at least, in my modest opinion – far more than charming feminine rumps seem actually improved by a few strokes of the birch. Anyhow, this scene displeased me and I took refuge in my hut. I had intended to return that night and try to speak to Frank, but slept very heavily and awoke only when it was broad daylight and already hot.

In spite of this stifling heat it rained until the start of the afternoon. The hills with their shaggy fleece of greenery and the lofty blue ridge of mountains weighed massively upon my heart as if I were never to see them again. Frank remained cloistered in his hut, captive perhaps, of his own amazement – as he had been, in my view, from the first. Everything was repeating itself – the only difference being that *I* now felt quite free. As I have said, my heart felt heavy, heavier than the drowsiness which had afflicted me, and yet inside myself I knew a joy as light as a bird's. The drizzle stopped, the bush smouldered on in its dull fever and the hills shimmered. Then Frank was brought out of his hut. They led him to the edge of the great meeting-place cleared out of the undergrowth, to a bed built up like the vaulting-frame, whose top was hump-backed. The women were on one side of this, while that day Ra-Hau of his own accord had requested the children to keep back. Of course there being no actual taboo in force, the injunction was only half-heartedly obeyed, and at every moment small groups of the curious did not neglect to worm their way forward so as to enjoy the spectacle.

Frank, stripped to the buff, was placed upon the bed, first of all lying on his stomach. They were less confident of his servility than they had been of mine, and after spreadeagling him, had secured his wrists and ankles to each of the four corners of the bedstead. I myself remained in the vicinity; although not going and sitting on the edge of the bed with the women, nor did I slip away from the scene. I was still dressed in English style, which the smiles of the natives who looked at me seemed to approve, I do not know why.

Frank exploded into furious oaths as the women

began to depilate him around the backside, so they stuffed a sort of mango with a big hard pip between his teeth to serve as gag. Perhaps one hour later, not only the crease between his buttocks but also the cheeks themselves were as naked and smooth as a baby's. There was a striking contrast with the black hair on the backs of his thighs, which had been spared, and with the long line of hair running down the middle of his back, along the spinal column, neatly finishing at the last vertebra. I no longer know why this contrast seemed rather exciting. Then the young women, just as they had done with me, undertook to massage his hinder parts, gradually sinking their fingers into his arsehole and employing the various oils which prevent or soothe irritation. I then went to sport with Ta-Lila, Nawa-Na, and others in the big hut. Apparently Nawa-Na did not set to work when a man was involved. But there was no question of a taboo there either, since the women depilating and massaging Frank were no older than she, nor were they all married.

When I came back to see him he was lying on his back, still tied of course, and arched up because of the bed's hump. His groin had been subjected to the same artistic handiwork (if I can call it that) as his jacksy, and previously, as my own pubis and vulva. From navel to thigh the women had left not the shadow of a hair. The seals themselves had been most carefully shaved. They how resembled small, lightly browned and slightly wizened eggs. At the time I thought I had never seen anything so droll as that tender and unfortunate penis and those miserable bald eggs. It were as though they had actually just been grafted or added on to Frank's body like an extravagant baroque ornament.

The women, who had already oiled and massaged his belly and cock were now busy with his testicles. By the looks of it the depilatory process had much inflamed them, and they were now wrapped by the women in a whole variety of leaves, mosses and grass steeped in different unguents. When the women finally uncovered them they seemed to have lost their clearly swollen demeanour and the rather empurpled, congested redness. I also noted that the fruit gagging Frank's mouth had been removed. His jaw muscles were so tense that he was in effect serving to gag himself. The drollness and even absurdity of this wretched, denuded and despoiled engine must have struck him too, and intensely what is more, so that one could not help but be touched: this last sentiment for me at any rate, also included a no less intense feeling of excitement.

Involuntarily I approached the bed. The women looked up and smiled at me proudly, quite as happy with their labours as they had been when the same was done to me. Frank, on the contrary, met my gaze with a look that burned with a crazed, wild hatred. But it left me unmoved, for my own eyes kept returning to his privates – to those grotesque and adorable little bollocks. The women retired, making way for me to sit down amongst them upon the bed. The transparent layer of oil upon Frank's loins and privates was bothering me as it continued glistening in the sun. I had only to stretch out my hand and one of the young women proffered a scrap of very dry, soft material, finer than flax. I busied myself with getting rid of the last traces of this oily concoction. Indeed I found it highly agreeable, dressed from head to toe myself as I might have been at teatime in England, to treat him thus, who was not only naked but deprived of the scanty and modest little defences nature affords. Under the effect of such thoughts, my own sex seemed to quiver, to palpitate voluptuously beneath my garments. At that moment I was wiping Frank's pego, taking care not to aggravate the irritation, and as I held it cautiously in my palm I felt it stir, grow heavier, then begin to stand. Frank, despite his attempts to contain himself, burst out:

'For God's sake don't do that!' he hissed.

'Why not?' I said.

I threw away the rag. The shaft appeared in all its nudity, erect and rigid as a lance. Frank suddenly flushed then turned pale with fury and hate. As I had once done myself, he closed his eyes tightly to hide from the world by denying it. But it is only too true to say that his feelings scarcely mattered to me just then. The young women laughed, some of them clapped their hands and began chattering, while the men who had arrived muttered, for their part, with evident satisfaction. I think the natives very much like nature to take its course.

'Devil take you, you damned bitch, you filthy slut, you whore!' Frank spat out.

I grasped him without brutality yet firmly, and frigged him as I had never frigged anybody, not even Ra-Hau nor one of the young lads when I wanted them to service me and they were showing reluctance. Alas, it took only seconds – far too brief for my liking and far too insubstantial if not intangible – for the member to rear upright in my hand, its knob all swollen, flowering a fine purplish-pink, and to eject in a series of violent spasms its essence, shooting it under Frank's chin and into the hollow of his collarbone. The women exclaimed delightedly and applauded in earnest. Frank was washed and dried. As soon as he was dry I started frigging him again. This time it took longer, and if his spasms were more ferocious, the jets were not so forceful nor so copious.

'Slut! Slut!' Frank repeated.

But this time it was well-nigh a groan. Why not? I thought. More than ever I was fascinated by the neat play of the pills which would now tightly contract below the shaft as if to serve it as flying-buttress, now relax, spread and slither slowly against each other like well-seasoned billiard balls in a fine leather pouch. Without stretching the truth I may say that I had never seen Frank entirely in the altogether.

I let the women take their time wiping, washing and drying him again. One of the men brought him some water in a shell. Frank drank it with his head averted, not looking at me. Then after a few tranquil moments had elapsed beneath the warm shadow of the trees, I grasped his prick again and began frigging it once more. A second later his whole body arched convulsively as if to escape at a stroke both my fingers and the touch of the leafy mattress, and Frank gave vent to a low groan. Between his stubbornly closed eyelids I saw oozing a moisture or dampness which might have been tears perhaps, or simply perspiration. I only manustuprated him with redoubled vigour. A man too should be turned inside out like a rabbit skin or a glove. And if he has not been, what can he know of pleasure? Or what can he know of others and of himself?

I must have worked at that unfortunate phallus for an incredible length of time before sensing the pulsation of ecstasy course through it from root to knob. But although it twitched and jerked like a mad thing, it finally emitted only a minute quantity of fluid, curiously flecked with blood. And yet this poor ejaculation tore from Frank's chest (and, one might even have imagined, his belly) such a strangled moan, such a coarse, agonised yell, that it might have been assumed, again, that he was giving birth or at least fertilising a very mountain. I had to allow that I would extract nothing further from him. His whole body had collapsed, and I suppose his spirit had too. I kept in my hand what had been a weapon, until it had once again turned into a pitiful, charming little penis. Even its tiny gluey emunction no longer repelled me. When the women had washed and dried him I leaned over and slipped it for just a second inside my mouth, simply to feel its weight and soft warmth. Then I stood up once more and went away with Ra-Hau and Ta-Lila.

As I had done, so Frank, for several days more, greatly diverted the natives, especially the women. Whether in public or in the privileged retreat of the huts they vied with each other in violating him - to the very limits of his capacities, to be precise. They knew very well, banding together in groups if he showed reluctance, how to make him rise even while he was defiantly gnashing his teeth, and would then straddle him one way or another, stuffing his shaft into their sphincters or their sexes.

The young girls adored him, frigging and mumbling him to the point where he was drained and glassy-eyed. I never joined in all this, finding it absurd to deprive him of all these pleasures. My life, after all, went on. I believe the younger women and girls flogged Frank on different occasions, and they also sodomised him from time to time, doubtless for a change, though without any males being involved. They would insert into his arse the customary fruits. And again, why not? My own indisposition had been forgotten long ago, and once again I went about dressed in my loincloth, or often quite naked. I recall that Frank changed colour the first time he set eyes on my medlar, itself as smooth and naked as his own sex.

Time had fragmented, however. There had been some break in the chain, some split, and its course seemed to miss a beat or falter while flowing through my veins. A few days, indeed a very few days, after Frank's reappearance I understood: I knew for certain that he, Frank, would never resort to wandering naked around the *pah* as I did, nor interest himself with its life, times and history, or its absence of history, if one prefers.

That made me sorry. In the middle of the night I went to see him in the hut which had tacitly become his. One of my girl friends, slender and naked, was lying beside him, her cheek resting upon his folded arms, and her buttocks spread. The starlight lent her brown skin a delicate sheen. Frank himself was not asleep: I saw his eyes shine. He propped himself nervously upon one elbow as I sat down on the leafy mattress, and also seemed unconcerned about waking the young native girl. I stroked her softly, happy to smell the distinctive warm aroma of her parts. She clung to her sleep like a small animal. I was wearing a shift and in the darkness I distinguished an involuntary movement by Frank to conceal his own nakedness.

'Stella,' he said at last.

'Yes.'

'Help me, and I too will assist you. We must succeed in making our escape.'

A long silent moan seemed to sound within my very soul.

'Very well, Frank,' I said.

'Do you think we have a chance? Yes, of course, there's always a chance. We'll get the better of these bastards! Do you know where they've hidden the clothes they stole from me?'

'I shall find them,' I said, again wearily.

Frank looked anxiously at the crudely-fashioned door, then at the native girl I was caressing.

'Fitzimmons, the new Major, has established an advance post just the other side of Waikato. It is impossible for these jackals to dislodge him, and by walking all night we'll join up with him again. We might even find horses. Two or three from my squadron bolted when that scum ambushed us.'

'Very well, Frank.'

'Go and get dressed now. Proper clothes, mind! - And fetch me mine. Don't forget the boots, but just make sure the spurs don't jingle. We'll do it, you'll see.'

He made a sardonic grimace.

'What a rabble, eh! Didn't even bother posting sentries.'

'Yes Frank,' I said.

I have just finished writing these lines in that same manor buffeted by the wind. How many centuries has it remained thus? How many more centuries will it remain, unchanging, unmoved? One must grow very old oneself not in order to learn, but simply to assess the force of habit. My husband Frank is close by, presently swilling French wines with his comrades, sequestered within the thick walls of the hunting lodge. Sudden squalls of wind and rain bear the smell of the sea. I am happy, because everybody is. From time to time on other nights, Frank and I make love - above all when *he* wishes to do so. First, we must doff shift and nightshirt.

I have concealed this account from Frank by covering all the preceding pages. Now, once again, listening for a sound, a door opening, I hold myself

137

Oh Wicked Country

in readiness, I hide. From what? That I do not know. No doubt from Frank. From the whole world. From myself, perhaps. *Out there* I never used to hide.

Wicked, yes ... Oh wicked country!